BORN TO FLY

BORN TO FLY

The Heroic Story of Downed U.S. Navy Pilot Lt. Shane Osborn

SHANE OSBORN

with Malcolm McConnell
adapted for young people by Michael French

A Dell Yearling Book

Published by
Dell Yearling
an imprint of
Random House Children's Books
a division of Random House, Inc.
New York

Copyright © 2001 by S.D. Sugar Inc.
Map created by Rick Britton

Visit us on the Web! www.randomhouse.com/kids

Educators and librarians, for a variety of teaching tools, visit us at www.randomhouse.com/teachers

---

ISBN: 0-440-23796-3

Reprinted by arrangement with Delacorte Press

Printed in the United States of America

October 2003

10 9 8 7 6 5 4 3

OPM

prologue

On April 1, 2001, in the cold predawn darkness, my crew and I hurtled down the long runway of Kadena Air Base in our large gray and white U.S. Navy aircraft and lifted into a star-filled sky. Kadena is an American air base on the Japanese island of Okinawa, and both our navy and our air force routinely fly peacetime missions from there. With stable, clear weather, the land soon disappeared below us, and we swept over the South China Sea for our routine nine-hour surveillance and intelligence-gathering mission in international airspace.

I had no idea that those routine nine hours would not be so routine on this Sunday. Not even the fact that it was April Fools' Day gave me an inkling that I was in for the most death-defying adventure of my relatively young life—or anyone's life, for that matter.

I was mission commander on our EP-3E ARIES II, a relatively slow-moving aircraft that bristled with pods and sensors and was powered by four turboprop engines. About six hours after takeoff, when we were ready for the last leg of our mission before returning to Kadena, my crew and I were suddenly intercepted by a pair of Chinese fighter pilots. In their sleek, fast gray jets, they darted in and out at us without concern for anyone's safety.

Being harassed by the Chinese fighters was nothing new to EP-3E pilots. This had happened on other missions over the last few months, and my crew and I had encountered the same type of behavior only the week before. But now one aggressive Chinese pilot swung his fighter too close to the left wing of our EP-3E. Much too close.

In another instant, the jet struck one of our propellers. Seconds later, his plane was cut in half.

Sitting in the pilot's seat on the right of the EP-3E, I heard a sickening crunch and felt our plane shudder violently. Some of the crew was screaming. When I looked out my overhead window, I saw the Chinese jet was in bright flames, hurtling toward the ocean.

And our plane was in free fall right behind it.

There were twenty-four of us on board the EP-3E ARIES II, and everyone scrambled to their emergency position on the plane. No matter what we were feeling inside, we each had a job to do.

The navy had drilled us in so many emergency procedures that the training had sometimes seemed excessive. Now, as some of the dials on my instrument panel spun out of control, I knew otherwise. Falling from the sky at over 300 miles per hour, with my brain and heart moving almost as fast, I would need everything the navy had taught me to save our plane and the lives of my crew. I was a navy pilot—a role I had been preparing for my entire life.

chapter one

Becoming a pilot had been my dream and ambition for as long as I can remember. Flying in a small Piper Cub, in fact, was one of my first vivid memories. I was three years old and living with my mother, Diana, my father, Doug, and my older sister, Lynnette, in a tiny South Dakota town named Loomis. The population of Loomis was around fifty if you didn't count anything with four legs. Besides the houses in our neighborhood, there were just a general store, a church, a grain elevator, and a one-room schoolhouse. Loomis had once been busier and more prosperous, but when the railroad abandoned the town, most businesses dried up like tumbleweeds.

The folks who remained there were solid and decent. One of our neighbors, a sheep farmer named Lyle Brewer, flew a bright yellow Piper J-3 Cub out of a pasture near our house. Lyle, who had been a pilot his whole adult life, had bought the Piper from a military surplus catalog and assembled it in his barn. Although I don't remember this very well, my dad says I tried to visit Lyle whenever I knew he was working on his plane.

I took my first flight with Lyle and Dad almost as soon as the FAA inspector signed the airworthiness certificate for the Piper, stating that the plane was safe to fly. That experience I definitely do remember. After I got strapped in on Dad's lap in the narrow rear seat, Lyle hit the starter. A puff of smoke belched from the engine, and the wooden prop fluttered to life. Lyle opened the throttle, and the plane began to shake as it bounced down the bumpy pasture. The tail wheel lifted off the grass just as we reached a little dip, and we gained airspeed on the downslope. Seconds later, the ground dropped away and we were climbing into the sky.

"How do you like it, Shane?" Dad yelled to me over the roar of the engine. From the ear-to-ear grin on my face, I'm sure he already knew the answer.

"We're flying!" I shouted back.

The Piper Cub had hinged windows that folded down and opened. When Dad freed them and loosened our seat belt, I immediately leaned over to get a better view.

"Whoa," he said, keeping his arm around my chest. The view of the earth passing slowly below captured my senses: square fields of green alfalfa, twisting ribbons of cottonwood trees, and rows of tasseled corn that always seemed so tall on the ground but looked like grass from above. I could smell the ripening crops and clapped with pleasure.

Lyle turned south and began to climb again. I flattened my hand like a little airplane and pretended to be flying, my body an extension of the Piper Cub. Then I hunched over Lyle's shoulder to gaze at the instrument panel and see what Lyle was doing to fly the plane. It was even more fascinating than the view out the window. He had one hand on the throttle and the other on the control stick between his knees. His scuffed boots rested on a pair of rudder pedals.

As Lyle pulled back on the stick, I felt the nose (the cone-shaped front of the Piper) pull up. When he moved the stick to the right, the plane banked in the same direction; the right wing dipped down as the left wing rose. So this was how you flew an airplane, I thought, eyeing the second set of controls that were in the rear by Dad and me. I touched them gently as they moved in tandem with Lyle's movements up front.

"I want to fly," I told my dad.

"Not today, Shane."

When Lyle took us over the lake, I looked down at the miniature water-skiers carving white curves in the water. Before this flight, I'd always thought of the water-ski boats with their howling motors as the fastest, most powerful machines in the world. From up here they looked like toys. As we began to drift down through the afternoon sunlight, I felt a deep sense of satisfaction. This was better than any carnival loop-the-loop ride.

Takeoff had been a thrill, but landing was pure magic. It was as if we were pulling the whole huge earth into the sky. The left wheel hit the grass first, followed by another jolt from the right wheel. The tail wheel landed last, and I felt the cockpit sink back as our speed began to slow. After 300 feet, Lyle turned the plane and taxied over to his big red barn. I sat for a moment in my seat, reliving in my mind the power and beauty of the flight.

That summer I sneaked away from our house whenever I could to watch Lyle working on his plane in the barn. If my parents wanted to find me, they always knew where to look. Lyle was patient and always answered my questions. Sometimes he used a pencil to draw on a scrap of butcher paper, showing me the relationship between engine power and the airflow over the curved surface of the wings. By the age of four, I already had a basic understanding of lift and was beginning to learn how the aileron controlled the plane's angle of bank or roll, the elevator governed the degree of lift, and the rudder directed the sideways movement.

Whenever Dad could get off work, Lyle not only invited us to fly in his Piper Cub but let Dad and me sit in front while he steered the plane from the rear seat. Dad, a Vietnam vet who had been a forward observer for the artillery branch of the army, had begun to tell me war stories, so my imagination took over once I was in the front of Lyle's plane. Sometimes I pretended I was fighting in a war, and other times I imagined I was gliding over mountains or an ocean. Lyle would let me wrap my hand around the stick while he banked the plane left or right. I wasn't steering it, but I could feel that special connection between the pilot and his airplane.

After that summer, there was no doubt in my mind that I would be a pilot when I grew up. That early determination would be put to plenty of tests in the years to come, but my dream never changed.

To support our family, my mom and dad ran several small businesses in nearby Mitchell, a much larger town than Loomis, with a population of 8,500. Although Mom was a registered nurse, she and Dad felt they could make more money from their bookstore, upholstery, and pizza parlor businesses than a nursing job. My sister, Lynnette, and I stayed back in Loomis. While Lynnette attended the one-room schoolhouse, I was looked after by a neighbor.

I was definitely not a quiet child. When I wasn't flying, I was constantly in motion exploring the world. I don't remember being afraid of anything—which sometimes got me into trouble. When I was only one and beginning to walk, I stepped right into the deep end of a friend's swimming pool, even though I didn't know how to swim. Luckily, I was rescued, though that scare didn't slow me down. Around three years of age, I pushed my toy cart out the back door, down our driveway, and right onto the emergency lane of the nearby highway. I kept going, ignoring the traffic that whizzed by me.

While Mom and Dad worked long hours in Mitchell, Lynnette became my substitute mom after school. She was only four years older than me, but she made sure I kept my room clean, helped me get ready for church every Sunday, read to me, taught me to count, disciplined me if I misbehaved, and protected me from any kind of danger. As we got older, we had our differences, like any brother and sister, but they never weakened the strong bond that was formed during these early years.

Unfortunately, when I was five my parents began to feel the strain of running so many businesses on top of raising a family. Worse, Dad, who had seen the horrors of war and earned a Purple Heart for being wounded, had too many traumatic memories from Vietnam. As the tensions at home increased, my parents agreed to a divorce.

Mom took Lynnette and me back to her hometown of Norfolk, Nebraska, where Dorothy, her mother, still lived nearby. Norfolk was only three hours from Mitchell, and as a larger town with a population of about twenty thousand, it provided more activities for my sister and me. My dad was going to live in the same town, to be close to us, and for a while he did. But for his own reasons he moved on to a small town in Minnesota, and I didn't see him again for six years.

The divorce, and our family's physically breaking apart, was painful for me, but I knew I couldn't change things.

As we drove away from Loomis in a farm truck borrowed from my mom's brother, Uncle Bud, I kept my eyes fixed on the highway in front of us, wondering what my next adventure would be.

chapter two

Once we were settled in an apartment in Norfolk, Mom took a nursing job at the local Veterans Administration home. For extra income she tended bar at the country club and another place in town. She was usually exhausted when she got home at the end of the day, and took a short nap before starting her night job, but she never complained or felt sorry for herself. Our family needed the money, and she was determined that we would not suffer. Her example taught Lynnette and me that we would have to work hard to achieve what we wanted in life.

While I missed Lyle and my other friends in South Dakota, I was thrilled to be starting kindergarten in a "real" school, instead of going to Loomis's one-room schoolhouse. I loved everything about Northern Hills Elementary, especially the brightly colored maps of the world that hung on the classroom walls. Those were the countries I'd fly to when I was a pilot. And I sure had not forgotten that dream. Whenever anyone asked what I wanted to do when I grew up, my answer was always the same: "I'm going to be a pilot."

I was just a skinny little kid from a small town in South Dakota, with a struggling single mom, and making new friends wasn't easy, but my teacher, Ms. Anderson, made me feel right at home. Lynnette had already taught me how to count to a hundred, do some addition, and recite the alphabet. Besides introducing me to my new classmates, Ms. Anderson quickly recognized my gifts for math, science, and reading, and she didn't hesitate to push me in those directions. I loved the challenge. I always went to school early and tried to get a perfect score on every assignment.

Until the chicken pox kept me home for a few weeks, I was proud of my perfect attendance and couldn't stand being out of school. Ms. Anderson cried and gave me a big hug when I returned, and I quickly made up any missed assignments. I was incredibly happy to be back. Some of my friends complained about being bored with class work, while others were given money by their parents whenever they brought home a good grade. Neither practice made much sense to my mom. She believed that it was my job to study hard and do well, not because I got money for it but because I loved what I was learning. And I did love it.

After I finished second grade, we moved from our apartment to a small ranch house in nearby Woodland Park. It was the most basic of houses, but I loved our neighborhood because there were twenty-eight kids my age on my street alone. It was a safe area, and we could roam as a pack or individually, exploring the nearby woods and creek to our heart's content. We also liked to play war with our collection of plastic G.I. Joe figures, building imaginative forts and orchestrating battle scenes that would go on for hours, if not entire weekends.

At my new school, Grant Elementary, I set my goals even higher than at Northern Hills, determined not to miss a day even if I was sick. By the third grade I was placed in advanced reading and math, and in a matter of weeks I completed a year's worth of curriculum. My math and science teacher, Mrs. Monroe, asked me to be her assistant by helping classmates who were falling behind and by grading student papers. I did whatever I was asked, not caring if other kids called me the teacher's pet. I was lucky to have such good teachers so early in my life—they were incredible role models. They taught me what it meant to be dedicated to your profession, and they encouraged me to study hard. This became a lifelong habit for me, and it would serve me well in my navy pilot training. While I had lots of friends to spend time with after school and on the weekend, my first priority was doing well in school.

Summers were a different story. I wouldn't visit Dad

and his new wife, Julie, at his home in Minnesota until I was eleven, so Mom sent me to her brothers' hog farm near Platte Center, just south of Norfolk, for several consecutive summers. My uncles, Bud and Mike, put me to work walking beans and chopping out the weeds under the hot prairie sun. It was tedious, backbreaking labor, and the stable flies wouldn't leave anyone alone. At first I was so miserable, I wanted Mom to take me back to Norfolk, where I could spend my time reading or riding my chopper bike. But my two cousins, Uncle Bud's son, Junior, and Uncle Mike's boy, Rich, worked the bean fields too and never complained, even though they didn't like the work any more than I did.

Rich and Junior became close friends of mine. Everyone in their two families were strong individuals who had a clear sense of who they were. Maybe it helped being from midwestern farm stock, where self-reliance was a way of life, but I realized during those summers that I had those qualities too. Besides being self-reliant, everyone in those families was a good judge of character, able to size up both friends and strangers quickly and accurately. I fit right into the mold. Working long hours day in and day out in those bean fields provided still another valuable lesson: You learned something about your strengths and weaknesses when you stuck to a job you hated.

Back in Norfolk, around my tenth birthday, I traded in my chopper bike for a Yamaha GT-80 dirt bike. The engine was small, but the thrill of racing over dusty trails to the Elkhorn River after school and on weekends was as magical as my first ride in Lyle's Piper Cub. It was illegal for kids under sixteen to ride motorized bikes on public streets, and when the cops caught me they would give me a warning. They didn't want to go to my mom because they knew she worked three jobs and didn't need more aggravation in her life.

Eventually, however, Mom found out, and she and I had an open talk that I'll never forget. "Shane," she said one night after dinner, "I trust you and Lynnette, and I trust your judgment. I don't have the time to be looking over your shoulder. All I'm asking is for you to be responsible, do well in school, and stay out of trouble."

I felt bad for having done something I shouldn't have but proud that Mom would still put her trust and confidence in me. It made me feel grown-up, and I promised that I wouldn't let her down.

One of my favorite weekend activities was visiting the men in the Veterans Administration home where Mom worked. Most of the residents were in their sixties and seventies and had served in World War II, but some were even older and had fought in World War I. I understood a little about what my dad had gone through in Vietnam, but our country's earlier wars were a mystery to me. My imagination was fired by the vets' stories about German airplanes and World War II battles in Europe and in the Pacific. Some of the men made models of planes and wanted me to have them. I was flattered by their kindness. Back home, I hung all of these models from my ceiling with fishing wire to create a floating battlefield complete with aerial support.

One of the residents named Bill made me a model of the battleship U.S.S. *Arizona*. He told me how it sank at a place called Pearl Harbor and thousands of men drowned inside the battleship. This was how I began to learn about World War II and what it meant to be a veteran as well as a patriot. War had never been a game for these vets. They had risked their lives to serve their country, and many others had died for it. Now hardly anybody came to visit them. I made up my mind then that I would stop by the VA home as often as possible. It was the least I could do to honor their service.

About this time, my mom's boyfriend, Jerry Williams, moved in with us. He had five children of his own, and though they lived with his ex-wife for most of the year, they came by a lot in the summers. Jerry's second-youngest son, Tony, and I became particularly close because we both loved exploring, camping, and riding bikes. During their visits, our small house would suddenly become a whirlwind of activity. When Mom laid down new household rules, Jerry expected us to follow them. I was almost a teenager now, and my sense of humor was often sarcastic. Jerry would let me know when I was out of line. He was friendly but strict, and I respected his authority at a time when I needed a father figure in my life.

Before I entered junior high, I was getting tall but

hadn't filled out much. That worried me, partly because I cared about my appearance and partly because I didn't want to be picked on. There were boys my age whose biceps were bigger than my thighs, and they could be cruel. One said I looked like a poodle with my curly, sun-bleached hair. I began lifting weights with the same discipline I tried to bring to every challenge I accepted. After a year, I was proud of the muscle I'd put on, and I didn't worry about kids picking on me anymore.

I also asked my mom for permission to get a job after school and on weekends. I wanted to start taking responsibility for my life and to earn some extra spending money. There was one store in Norfolk, called Brass Buckle, that carried the "in" jeans—one brand was called Pepe, and another was Guess—and every kid, including me, had to have them. Every fall, if I was lucky, Mom would buy me one pair of Pepe jeans, and they had to last for the entire year. When she agreed to let me work as a busboy at the local Village Inn as long as I maintained good grades, I began to have money for a few small luxuries.

My life became very busy, which was how I liked it. Studying, lifting weights, participating in sports, working as a restaurant busboy, doing chores at home—I didn't have too many free moments. As busy as I was, though, I never gave up my unofficial volunteer duty hanging out with the vets at the VA home. Now that I knew so much more about the sacrifice they'd made for America, I considered it an honor just to be in their company. You never knew if some quiet new-comer sitting in the corner of the dayroom had won the Medal of Honor in the Normandy invasion or spent three years as a prisoner of war in the Pacific.

I also kept my eyes and ears open for new challenges. One afternoon at school when I was twelve, a woman named Mrs. Askew give a presentation on the Civil Air Patrol (CAP), an auxiliary branch of the U.S. Air Force. I listened intently to every word.

The CAP was organized something along the lines of the Boy Scouts, which I'd been involved with since second grade. By then I had almost enough merit badges to become an Eagle Scout. I probably would have earned that honor if not for what I learned about the CAP that afternoon. The Scouts were great, but in the CAP you learned how to fly—and you could earn your pilot's license by your sixteenth birthday.

When Mom got home from work that night, I told her how much I wanted to join. There was a $40 fee, and you had to invest $140 in uniforms. This was money we could barely afford.

She looked at me a long time. "You really want this, don't you, Shane?"

"I sure do, Mom."

She sat down at the kitchen table and wrote a check.

The Civil Air Patrol absorbed me completely. For the first time since starting school, I was distracted from my studies, at least in the beginning. I soon realized, though, that the CAP made me want to study even harder than before. We had after-school classes in the history of flight, fundamental aeronautics, and space travel, and there were tests on what we learned in those classes. You advanced in rank depending on both your test score and your progress in military training. Discipline in one area, I began to see, was directly related to progress as a would-be aviator. The reward for that progress was getting to fly in our squadron's Cessna 172.

The more skills I acquired, the more airtime I was given. One of the CAP's primary responsibilities is searching for downed aircraft, triangulating their position from the beeps of their emergency locator transmitter radio beacon. To master this, the other cadets and I dug in hard to the demanding tasks of map reading and applied geometry. Because of my math skills, I found this challenge relatively easy. As I'd done back in elementary school, I also had the satisfaction of helping friends in my squadron master this process.

The first of my four years in the CAP, I tried to sharpen my military image, which was undoubtedly the weakest aspect of my squadron work. Mom taught me how to press sharp creases into my uniform, and when I visited Dad at his new home near Minneapolis, he showed me the finer points of how to get a shine on my boots.

But there was still the problem of my hair. Although

it was short enough on the sides to meet regulations, I had a narrow tail that I usually tucked under my collar. After drill, when the cadets went to hang at Daylight Donuts, some kidded me that I'd never make rank wearing my rattail. I loved the haircut because it was in style. But I also realized that keeping my tail might get in the way of advancing in the CAP and even jeopardize my chance to earn a private pilot's license. Nothing was going to get in the way of that. I cut my hair. Shortly after, I even became a drill instructor.

I also accepted the challenge of studying to become a tornado spotter. This too was important community work because we lived in one of the most active tornado belts of the Midwest. When violent weather threatened in spring and summer, members of our squadron, equipped with handheld radios, were often dispatched along country roads. There we would watch for the telltale funnel clouds emerging out of the black mass of ominous thunderheads. It was a thrilling assignment.

Another duty I accepted was studying to become a warden of a nuclear bomb shelter. We had several in town, located in underground structures. Most had been built in the 1950s at the height of the Cold War, when a missile attack by Russia seemed like a real possibility. Nowadays, the shelters are largely designed for other emergencies, such as severe storms or tornadoes. By age fifteen, I was a certified warden, and found myself guiding state civil defense officials around my particular shelter.

There was one other aspect of the CAP that was important to me. I liked belonging to something that was bigger than myself, feeling connected to a group that was like a family. The military structure of the CAP and the close bonds I felt with other cadets provided a secure environment. And my work ethic was always rewarded. The better I did at my CAP studies, the more flight time I was given in our squadron's Cessna 172. My ultimate reward was a 400-mile overland flight down to Ogallala, Nebraska, and back. We flew out there for a CAP conference and to practice Search and Rescue. On both flights, I got to sit in the right seat and handle the controls under the supervision of the instructor pilot. By next year I'll be flying on my own, I thought.

Having goals has always been important to me. By the end of my sophomore year I had logged sixteen hours in the Cessna to help me qualify for a pilot's license. But then I hit a wall. The fees for additional training and the license were steep—even more than I could earn in my after-school job—and I didn't want to ask Mom for more money. She was working hard enough just to make ends meet. Besides, I had my distractions for the next year—football, playing electric bass guitar in a jazz band, and trying to master the tuba in the school band. I never did get my license. Still, I knew my CAP training was anything but in vain. I had learned a lot about flying and navigation, and I hoped my accomplishments in the CAP could eventually help me win an appointment to the U.S. Naval Academy at Annapolis. That had become my next long-term goal.

By the time I finished my junior year, my life felt totally organized. I couldn't have been in better spirits. Then, one night in July, something unimaginable happened that put my goal, and my life, in serious jeopardy.

chapter three

That July evening I had decided to drive down to Lincoln with Lynnette and her boyfriend, Tony Waugh, to visit Grandmother Dorothy, who'd just undergone hip surgery. Tony borrowed my mom's Nissan sedan, a cramped little car that was even more uncomfortable for someone with long legs like mine. In the passenger's seat, I unbuckled my seat belt, pushed the seat back as far as it could go, and tried to take a nap. Lynnette was already curled up asleep in the back. I suppose I should have been trying to keep Tony company, but I soon dozed off. I found out later that Tony had set the car's cruise control at sixty-five miles per hour, and without anyone to talk to on the flat prairie highway in the middle of the night, he had accidentally fallen asleep too.

Our Nissan plowed straight into the back of a

slow-moving John Deere tractor. The impact was so violent that our car broke the tractor's rear axle.

The driver of the tractor was thrown off his seat and into a ditch, but he wasn't hurt badly. The Nissan was crushed like a tin can. Without the restraint of a seat belt, my body flew forward, and my head slammed through the windshield. If my knees hadn't jammed into the firewall to stop my forward momentum, I'm sure I would have been thrown out of the car and probably killed instantly. The glass of the shattered windshield shredded my left eyelid and ripped my nose loose so that it flapped to one side, exposing bone and cartilage. Shards of glass were embedded in my scalp and sliced my face like razor blades. I'm thankful I don't remember the actual moment of collision, but my side of the car absorbed most of the impact.

When I woke up, I was lying back in my seat, listening to a medic's voice. I remember seeing the pulsing red strobe of the emergency lights.

"I think this one's dead," the medic said, meaning me.

As much as I tried, I couldn't answer because my lips were bruised and torn. I couldn't get a single sound out. Somewhere nearby I could hear Lynnette sobbing. I had no idea what had happened to Tony. My stomach was slowly filling with blood as it gurgled down my throat, and I groaned loudly before slipping back into unconsciousness.

When I woke again, I was in the emergency room of the hospital in David City. While a nurse held me down, a doctor was sewing my left eyelid into place. The trauma team had not given me an anesthetic because I had been unconscious, and they were afraid I'd suffered a serious concussion. Awake now, the pain was so extreme that I screamed from the bottom of my lungs. The doctor looked frightened and sent a nurse to find a couple of orderlies, who quickly restrained my arms with thick straps.

"Don't move," the doctor ordered me. "You'll just make it worse."

While I couldn't raise my arms because of the straps, I gripped the bed rail so hard that I bent the stainless steel.

When Mom came to see me that night, the doctor had just put in 220 stitches, and my face had swollen to twice its normal size. Incredibly, both Tony and Lynnette had survived the crash with only minor injuries. I was the one to occupy my mom's attention. As a trained nurse, she knew not to strain my emotions with this initial visit, so she didn't say much, but I could see in her eyes how disfigured I must have looked.

When she left, I asked one of the nurses to hand me a mirror. I gaped in horror at my reflection. I looked like something out of a monster movie—a bloated face, blackened flesh, a closed left eye, and a trail across my face of zigzagging stitches.

In the next few days, as the shock of that image began to wear off, a cold fear formed in my belly. The vision in my left eye was probably ruined. How would I ever become a military pilot? Maybe I'd never even qualify for a private pilot's license. I was sixteen years old, and I thought my life was over.

I spent the next month slowly healing in Lynnette's apartment in Lincoln, where she attended the University of Nebraska. I refused to entertain visitors because I didn't want pity. I worried about my looks and about whether I would be accepted back at school without people staring or whispering about me. Until I knew what I would look like, I wanted to be left alone.

But when Jerry's son Tony asked if he could visit, I relented. At Lynnette's apartment, he took one look at me and shook his head. "Man, Shane, you look really messed up."

When he left, all my anxieties about my left eye and a future in the military returned. I couldn't imagine losing my dream of flying.

As the summer dragged on, my bruised knees healed, and I underwent reconstructive surgery on my face that hid the worst of my scars. But my left eyelid was still a mess. The upper eyelashes of my left eye were tucked under the lid, sticking in, not out, so they constantly poked against my eyeball. After initial tests, my vision appeared to be normal, yet my ophthalmologist warned me that I would know for sure only after the eyelid had been permanently reconstructed.

Because I wanted to return to a normal life, I elected to postpone the surgery until after football season, with my doctors' approval. That fall I let out all my aggressions and frustrations on the field. No one worked harder than me that season. I went from third string to a starting position as wide receiver on offense and outside linebacker on defense. My self-esteem was slowly coming back.

Finally, that winter, shortly after football season was over, I had the surgery. The plastic surgeon did an outstanding job, and when the wound healed, I had a normal eyelid. The crucial eye exam after the surgery showed that my vision had not been damaged.

"Are you certain?" I asked the ophthalmologist.

"Your vision is perfect, Shane."

When Mom got home from work that night, the first thing she saw was my wide, confident grin.

That confidence was unshakeable now. I had learned a lesson about inner strength and not giving up, even under the most difficult of circumstances. God, I realized, had protected me through the terrible car accident. He must have had a purpose for my life, and it was as clear as crystal. My dream was back on track. I was going to fly.

My last year in high school, while still recovering from the car crash, I interviewed for both the air force and naval academies. I was partial to the naval academy because my mom had a cousin, Pierce Johnson, who was an admiral in the navy, and whenever I visited him I thought he was pretty grounded as a person. I refused, however, to ask Pierce to use his influence to get me into Annapolis. I wanted to make the cut on my own. I did well on the interviews as well as the tests, and I got some great letters of recommendation. My teacher for advanced math and advanced science was Grant Arment, a no-nonsense man who always came right to the point. Maybe that's why his letter of recommendation was only one sentence: "Shane Osborn will succeed in whatever he chooses to do. Sincerely, Grant Arment."

I'm sure his letter didn't hurt, but competition was fierce for the limited number of appointments allotted to the state of Nebraska. Other high school seniors were selected ahead of me.

The news crushed me, though the blow was softened by the unexpected offer of an appointment to the U.S. Military Academy at West Point. I was flattered, of course, and while the tuition would be free because this was a service academy, I knew that becoming an army officer was not going to help me become a pilot. The army didn't fly planes. I had to decline the West Point offer.

Once again I thought my dream was over. My eye had survived the car accident, and I had gained a lot of strength and courage from the ordeal, but how was I going to become a pilot? How would I afford college tuition wherever I ended up? Fortunately, my hard work paid off. About three weeks after missing the cut for Annapolis, the navy contacted me. Because of my test scores, the results of my interviews, and my high school grades, I was awarded a four-year

Naval Reserve Officers Training Corps (NROTC) scholarship to any school that offered the program. All my tuition, fees, and books would be paid for by the government. At the end of the program, I would be commissioned an ensign in the United States Navy. If I did especially well in the program, I might be able to select naval aviation as my branch of the service and eventually earn my wings of gold, the metal insignia that a military pilot proudly wears on his uniform.

When I told Mom and Jerry the news, they were both ecstatic for me. My mom was so overcome with joy, she couldn't help crying. She had worked so hard for so many years for me to reach this day. I also told them I was choosing the University of Nebraska at Lincoln. Like my sister, I would be a Cornhusker. Jerry, Mom, and I had a big dinner that night to celebrate.

In the morning, Mom marched over to the VA home and submitted her resignation. For fourteen years she had tolerated a domineering boss with whom she'd had a constant, draining personality conflict. Now, with her last child off to college on a full scholarship, she was free to leave.

I was on my way to making my dream a reality.

chapter four

My mom made a smart business decision just before I entered my freshman year at the university. With her savings, she made a down payment on a run-down three-story boardinghouse near the university's football stadium. The plan was that I would board for free and we would rent the other rooms to friends. This would cover the mortgage payments and perhaps make a small profit. But first my soon-to-be brother-in-law, Tony, and I had to invest sweat equity in the house by painting, installing drywall, and putting in new carpet. The place looked terrific when we were done, and we had no trouble renting out the rooms and even some additional parking spaces.

As anyone who has been to a Cornhusker football weekend can testify, school spirit is strong. While I spent time with my friends almost every Friday night through Sunday afternoon, during the week I was serious about academics. Math was my major, and I also took as many science courses as I could. The curriculum was a lot harder than in high school, but none of it overwhelmed me.

Besides my pride, I was motivated to do well by the terms of my NROTC scholarship. If my grades slipped below a B average, I could be washed out of the program and lose my scholarship. The goal of NROTC, not unlike the goal of the naval academy at Annapolis, is to produce well-rounded navy officers with professional and leadership skills. Our battalion consisted of three companies of midshipmen, from midshipman fourth class (freshmen) to first class (seniors). While we didn't receive the concentrated military training found at Annapolis, my fellow midshipmen and I were expected to attend weekly lectures and drill assemblies. We also mastered the navy's basic personnel structure and the complete inventory of ships. We were tested not just on names and numbers of ships but their functions and capabilities. In addition, we learned about missile systems of both our allies and adversaries. At every opportunity, I asked questions about the navy's air operations, particularly its fighter pilots. My ultimate goal was never far from my thoughts.

Leadership was one of the essential elements stressed in the NROTC program. As part of our training, midshipmen were given assignments that tested both individual judgment and teamwork. My four years with the Civil Air Patrol had showed me the importance of quick, decisive thinking and taught me how to communicate my thoughts to others. In one NROTC exercise in the gym, we were divided into small teams and told to build a high plank bridge between two sets of bleachers. Although the distance from the bridge to the wrestling mats on the floor was not too great, the plank seemed awfully narrow. We had to guide people from one end to the other by swinging them from ropes suspended from the ceiling. As each person crossed successfully, the assistants on the floor had to leave one by one. This rule meant that the last person would be left with no one to swing the ropes, so we had to identify the midshipman with the best balance and least fear of heights to volunteer for this position.

The ultimate lesson of that exercise was that we all needed each other for the mission to succeed, that everybody had strong and weak points, and that it was important to acknowledge both. Hiding behind an image, or pretending to be something you're not, was an invitation to disaster.

The relationship among all midshipmen in NROTC, whether you were a freshman or a senior, was a tight one. "We're all middies. We'll all get through this together" was our informal slogan. The bond was especially strong among the prospective pilots. We knew we would soon face the navy's toughest selection process, and we supported each other. There was no room for jealousy or rivalries.

When I was a sophomore, the midshipmen who were interested in flying visited the sprawling naval air station in Pensacola, Florida, site of aviation preflight indoctrination (API)—boot camp for navy pilots. We were excited about going through a few days of orientation, just to get a taste of the future. One morning we gathered in a nondescript building where a smiling petty officer introduced us to a strange-looking apparatus: a huge drum perched in the middle of the floor with thick electrical cables snaking out from underneath. Six narrow vertical cylinders, each big enough to accommodate a single person, were spaced evenly around the drum's inner wall. The instructor explained that the narrow cylinders rotated with the bigger drum, but they could also spin independently in the opposite direction, then reverse their spin when the drum changed direction.

"This little machine is called the spin-and-puke," the instructor said. "Anyone have an idea why?"

We all laughed nervously. The answer was clear. With the doors closed on both the smaller cylinders and the large drum, you lost all reference to the outside world.

"May I have six volunteers, please?" he said.

I marched right up with five of my other midshipman friends.

"Take a tube," the instructor said to us. "Doesn't matter which one."

I entered one and could immediately detect the faint ozone smell of electrical controls coming through the overhead air-conditioning vent. At least no one had gotten sick in this one, I thought.

The instructor closed all six cylinder doors. I felt the large drum move slowly to the right, while my tube also began to move. But was I moving right or left? My tube slowed and changed directions. Was I still moving right? It was impossible to tell. Then the speed increased, slowed, and increased again. I was getting more and more confused. The cylinder and drum kept weaving through this nauseating tango. One minute I was sure I was spinning to the right; the next thing I knew, I had stopped completely. If I blinked, it felt like I'd been moving steadily left all along. I'd been told to keep my eyes open to avoid getting sick, and maybe it helped. When we finally came to a stop, my stomach was less upset than a lot of my buddies'.

After everyone had done his turn with the spin-and-puke, the instructor told us how our sense of spatial orientation works. It depends on nerves, fluid-filled canals, and a collection of tiny, delicately balanced bones—all in our inner ear. When we cannot match the sense of motion with our visual reference points, he pointed out, we lose our equilibrium. This extremely hazardous condition can occur when pilots fly into clouds or when the horizon becomes obscured and they have no instruments, such as the gyroscope's artificial horizon or the vertical speed indicator, to orient them.

I knew from the CAP that the problem is called vertigo. It can kill you. You may think you're flying straight and level when in reality you are banking nose down or pitching up toward a stall.

"In a crisis, trust your instruments, not your senses," the instructor said. "Instruments never lie, but as you've just found out, your senses can fool you."

Another part of our orientation was to fly with an instructor in the navy's primary flight trainer, the T-34C Turbomentor. With straight wings, a bulging Plexiglas canopy, and two seats, the orange and white single-engine trainer resembled a World War II fighter. I was excited, hoping the instructor pilot, a lieutenant, might actually do some aerobatics once we were at a safe altitude.

But as he led me through a preflight inspection, the lieutenant seemed like a straight arrow who no doubt had more interesting things to do with the day than to take some overeager midshipman flying along the Gulf beaches. I couldn't have been more wrong. This was a guy who flat-out loved to fly. And he also loved sharing that joy.

Sitting behind the instructor pilot as we took off into a sparkling Florida sky, I relived those thrilling flights in Lyle Brewer's little Piper Cub all those years before. The T-34C was even more airplane. It was fully aerobatic, which meant it could fly the same maneuvers as the navy's hottest fighters, just a lot slower.

"How 'bout we try an aileron roll?" he suggested.

Before I could reply, he moved the control stick precisely 90 degrees to the right, and the plane was standing on its right wing. He rotated the stick another 90 degrees, and we were totally inverted. I was hanging in my harness looking up at the ocean.

"Feeling okay?" he asked mischievously.

"I feel great, sir," I said into my headset mike. This was the real-life equivalent of the spin-and-puke machine, and I loved every minute of it.

"Terrific," he said. "We'll do a couple of loops now."

The lieutenant hauled back on the stick. The plane's nose suddenly rose steeply above the horizon, and I felt as though I weighed a ton. This was so cool. I was experiencing G forces, or gravitational pull. For example, if you weigh 200 pounds, one G is the equivalent of 200 pounds. If you pull two G's, that's the equivalent of 400 pounds pressing down on you, and three G's would be 600 pounds. With that much pressure, it's difficult to move anything but your arms and legs, and even that feels like slogging through molasses. Fighter pilots, flying airplanes capable of very high speeds and complicated maneuvers, are trained to withstand up to six or seven G's.

We were briefly inverted again, and just when we seemed to pause in midair, the lieutenant took us into a steep dive. Then we did some more rolls and loops.

"This is just like being in the World War II films that we watched at NROTC assemblies," I told him.

He gave me a big grin. "Hey," he joked, "let's go strafe an enemy beachhead, then."

I had the ride of my life before we returned to Pensacola. Are all instructor pilots like this? I wondered. If they were, I wanted to go to flight school even more.

Little did I know.

As I entered my fourth year at the University of Nebraska, I realized I needed the equivalent of almost four semesters of a heavy credit load to complete my math major, specializing in statistics and actuarial science. In fact, it is common for people in this field to require five years to complete the degree. However, I was becoming increasingly impatient to graduate. I was now a midshipman first class in the NROTC program, but two of my best friends had already finished school, received their commissions as ensigns, and begun flight school. I had the choice of taking a normal number of credits and not graduating for another year and a half or doubling up on my workload and finishing by May 1996.

There was no doubt in my mind about what to do. Taking the slow track to anything was not in my nature. I took nineteen credit hours and then an incredible twenty-two hours my last semester. I never worked harder to keep my grades up, but by the spring, I had enough credits to graduate.

As good as I felt about earning my diploma, I now had to sweat out selection for flight school. Most midshipmen didn't make the cut for aviation and had to settle for another branch of the navy. Everybody who'd ever met me knew how badly I wanted to fly. In fact, the battalion skipper, Captain Stephen Delaplane, later told people, "Shane needs to fly like most people need to breathe."

So I was really nervous when our skipper called me into his office one afternoon. He had a grim look as he handed me a letter on Department of Navy stationery.

"Here are your orders, Shane," he said with a shake of his head. "I'm really sorry."

My eyes swept across the letter in disbelief. I was to report to the Pentagon annex and be assigned to a deputy who was the assistant to the coordinating chairperson of some committee I had never heard of.

I was stunned and speechless. Most of my buddies would be trying to qualify as fighter pilots, while I would be chained to a desk in the Pentagon annex.

When I looked up, I caught a twinkle in Captain Delaplane's eye. He didn't have the heart to stretch the prank any further.

"Shane, you got your pilot slot," he said as he pulled out my legitimate orders, smiling broadly. "You're going to Pensacola."

chapter five

I didn't have to report to Pensacola until October, so the summer was pretty much mine to do with as I pleased. Unquestionably, the highlight was a thirty-day cruise on the U.S.S. *Kitty Hawk,* which I boarded in San Diego with other NROTC midshipmen for our required summer duty. The 80,000-ton aircraft carrier was a finely tuned floating city of 5,000 navy men and women. As the *Kitty Hawk* churned through the frigid North Pacific waters, breaking the waves at 30 knots, my favorite activity was watching from the observation deck as F-14 Tomcats and F/A-18 Hornets took off and landed.

Crewmen in different-colored jerseys that identified their specialties scurried about within inches of the big fighters' engines. Planes were continually in motion, and you had to watch your back. Being blown down the flight deck by the jet wash of an F-14 on takeoff would not be a pretty picture.

When I was invited to take part in several catapult launches, first in a backseat of an EA-6B Prowler electronic warfare jet, then in an S-3B Viking patrol bomber, I thought again of my first ride with Lyle in his Piper Cub. If Lyle could only see me now, I thought. To be strapped tightly in your seat, staring out at the gray-black flight deck as the engines screamed, revving up to full military power just before the steam-powered catapult piston fired and flung your plane in the air . . . life didn't get any better. It was like being in the movie *Top Gun*, only this was real—and better.

On a carrier, a plane went from standstill to liftoff in about two seconds. That's the time it takes to snap your fingers twice. The noise and energy of the launches were overwhelming. If takeoffs were an example of pure thrust and speed, landings were a test of pinpoint accuracy and stomach-churning courage. A 30-ton F-14 Tomcat, for example, had a crooked steel tailhook hanging from its fuselage. The pilot would drop out of the sky and onto the flight deck, almost as if deliberately trying to crash his plane. Then its hook would snag one of the 4-inch-thick arresting cables, and the plane would lurch to a violent stop. If the pilot hit the deck too far forward of the cable or missed it on the backside, he had about one second to throw his throttle to afterburner, scream down the remaining length of the flight deck, and take off again. If he hesitated, his plane could easily stall and crash into the ocean. The pilot would then have to eject and his chute would open, with luck carrying him free of the carrier before the giant ship ran over him.

Watching their spectacular, risky takeoffs and landings, I was more determined than ever to become a navy pilot, just like them.

I ended my *Kitty Hawk* trip with a stopover at Pearl Harbor, where I visited the memorial erected over the sunken U.S.S. *Arizona*. As I recalled all the World War II stories, particularly about the bombing of Pearl Harbor, that the vets at the Norfolk VA home had told me, I was deeply moved. I understood even more clearly what the veterans of our country's longest and most costly war had endured. A good soldier or sailor never prays for war, but I wanted my country always to be ready, just in case.

I was back in Nebraska the following week. On June 21, 1996, I was commissioned an ensign in the United States Navy by my mother's cousin, Rear Admiral Pierce Johnson. Everyone in our family was in town because Lynnette's wedding was the next day. By still another coincidence, June 21 was my twenty-second birthday, so we all celebrated deep into the night.

I was finally a navy officer. In two more years, if all goes well, I thought, I'll earn my wings of gold and become a navy pilot.

chapter six

On a humid October morning, I reported to Pensacola with twenty-nine other student officers for our aviation preflight indoctrination (API). We had already heard rumors that there was a 50 percent rollback in API, meaning that half of us wouldn't graduate from the intense six-week program without going through parts of it twice, and many would eventually be pushed out of aviation training altogether. I was determined to be in the successful half.

My first challenge was passing the exhaustive two-day navy flight physical, during which medics poked and prodded every square inch of my body. What made me most nervous was the eye exam. Even though I'd been reassured after my reconstructive surgery that my left eye was in excellent condition, the exacting navy tests involved much more than chart reading. They measured depth vision and peripheral vision, as well as the curvature of each eye, both internal and external, in order to find any imperfection or evidence of injury. This was critical because an injured eye might not be able to withstand high G forces in flight.

When I received the news two days later that I had passed all aspects of my physical, I felt tremendous relief. Some of my classmates weren't so fortunate. Many left Pensacola to be trained for other service in the navy.

The classroom curriculum for the API focused on aerodynamics, propulsion, and weather, subjects that really intrigued me. This was information we would soon put to practical use in primary flight training. There was lots of reading, homework, and tests, and we were expected to master the increasingly complex information the first time around. In addition, we took physical and water survival training. I considered myself in excellent physical shape from lifting weights since junior high school, but I was never an endurance runner. When our instructor told us that everyone had to run a mile and a half through sand and brush in under ten minutes, not once but twice, I wasn't sure I could do it. Somehow, I managed to finish just under the wire both times.

In our swim training classes, we learned the art of survival floating, lying on your back and fluttering your extended hands just enough to keep your face above the surface. Our final exam was to tread water in a swimming pool for five minutes while wearing a flight suit, a helmet, 10-pound steel-toed boots, gloves, and an SV-2 survival vest with the life preserver unit (LPU) uninflated. After four and a half minutes, my thighs were burning so badly, I thought I would pass out. When the instructor blew his whistle after five minutes, it felt like half an hour. And the test still wasn't over. We needed enough breath to inflate our LPUs. I barely made it.

Sometimes I wondered why we went through such torture. What were the chances of actually crashing into the ocean and having to survive? Though the odds were extremely small, our instructors were so intense that they made us think it was inevitable.

Next we went through the high-altitude chamber, a claustrophobia-inducing welded-steel tube that looked like a railroad tank car. Seated on benches, we wore oxygen masks while the instructors took us "up" to an altitude of 35,000 feet by depressurizing the chamber. Breathing pure oxygen in this harsh environment, I felt normal, perfectly aware of my surroundings. Then the instructors took us back "down" to 25,000 feet.

"Masks off," the loudspeaker ordered.

Now came the manual dexterity tests we'd been briefed on. The Pensacola Patty Cake was the most demanding. Like three-year-olds in preschool, we tried to pat the open palm of the man or woman next to us, alternating left and right hands. The first twenty seconds or so of this was no problem. Then my partner hit my left hand twice. Deprived of oxygen too, I stupidly followed his move, mistakenly thinking this was a good idea and that the rules had changed. Ninety seconds into the exercise, we both had to stop and then start again.

"Numbers ten and eleven," the instructor ordered, "masks back on." We had become hypoxic, or oxygen-deprived, thinking we were doing fine when we actually were delirious. That was another vital lesson: Don't underestimate the danger of high-altitude flight.

Our final week of water survival training involved two scary-looking pieces of machinery: the helo and Dilbert dunkers. The helo dunker looked like a big gray soft-drink machine lying sideways on a ramp above the lip of the swimming pool. It simulated the cabin of a helicopter. Inside, eight of us strapped ourselves into seats on either side, and then the helo lurched down a pair of rails and into the pool. We were completely submerged—and then it flipped upside down! Windows were purposely opened and water rushed in, flooding the cabin. While scuba divers waited outside the helo dunker in case anyone panicked and need to be rescued, we each had to calmly unstrap ourselves and feel our way to the exit hatch, holding our breath until we made it to the surface.

It wasn't too terrible—until we attempted the exercise wearing blacked-out goggles to simulate night conditions. This was much scarier. Once we were underwater and our cabin was flooded, we had to take a different route to the exit hatch. I lost orientation almost immediately, and felt other cadets with the same problem kicking me as they struggled to orient themselves. I'm not going to make it, I thought, certain I couldn't hold my breath long enough to find the escape hatch. I had to resist the urge to rip off my goggles and swim to safety. Holding back my panic, I managed to find the right route and made it to the hatch. We had to successfully negotiate the helo dunker at least four times in six attempts, or we would keep repeating this exercise. I was grateful to pass.

The Dilbert dunker, unlike the helo dunker, looked like the cockpit of a single-seat fighter, and it slammed down rails at a steep angle and flipped upside down once underwater. The cockpit was quickly flooded, and once again I had to disengage my harness and open the hatch to make my escape. This might have been more difficult if I hadn't already been exposed to the helo dunker. I had no trouble getting out, but I did end up with a noseful of harshly chlorinated water.

Our water survival training ended with parachute exercises out on the bay, where we were towed in the air by a parasail behind a powerful speedboat. When it was my turn, I reached 500 feet in the air before I dropped my towline and floated into the water. Shedding my harness before the chute canopy dragged me down, I treaded water as I'd learned in my earlier training, waiting for an H-3H Sea King helicopter to rescue me. When it finally came, the large chopper made a deafening roar. I craned my neck to watch as an inflated yellow rescue collar dropped toward me on a winch cable. I was fetched out of the water like a fish on a reel. It was quite a thrill.

For Christmas I went home to stuff myself with my mom's and my grandmother Dorothy's rich Nebraska cooking. After working so hard for six weeks, it was nice to take a break. When I returned to Pensacola to finish my API training, I learned that eighteen of our twenty-nine cadets would either be rolled back or sent to other schools in the navy. I was one of the lucky eleven survivors.

chapter seven

Survivor was an apt term for any aspiring fighter pilot in the navy or the air force. The challenges of API had been rigorous, but what I was expected to master in the next round, primary flight training, was even more difficult. Sent to Corpus Christi, Texas, I became part of the VT-27 training squadron, reputed to be the toughest training squadron in the navy. Ahead of me were four weeks of grueling ground training, then soloing and months of specialized flying curriculum in the T-34C Turbomentor, the same plane I'd been given a ride in as an NROTC midshipman.

That first month in ground school was tedious and exacting. We slogged through T-34C aircraft systems and familiarization in the classroom, and we used simulators called cockpit procedure trainers (CPTs) to learn all about the T-34C's systems, controls, and instruments and how to handle emergencies, ranging from engine fires and wing and propeller icing to sudden drops in fuel flow and loss of hydraulic pressure. Hour after hour, we went through engine start-up and shutdown checklists and practiced raising and lowering the flaps and landing gear. There was homework every night, and we were tested regularly. In a grading system that went from Above Average (Above) to Average to Below Average to—worse yet—Unsatisfactory (Down), I managed to score an Above on my first exam, but it was by the skin of my teeth.

In primary, you lived or died on your cumulative scored performance. Only a small percentage of primary cadets earned high enough grades (called Jet Grades) to become qualified to fly the F-14 Tomcat, the F/A-18 Hornet, or any of the other jet aircraft that I'd seen on the *Kitty Hawk*—and that's what I was sure I wanted to do. I recognized and accepted the competition I faced and was confident I could meet the challenge.

Instructors introduced us to basic information, then expected us to put that information into practice, each week building on what had come the week before. Mastering emergency procedures depended on that foundation. While the final test of ground school was conducted in a simulator, the scenarios we faced were as real as the ones we might experience in any fighter cockpit. I was relieved when I received an Above, though I knew that the grades that counted the most were those you earned in the air or in simulators during the next and best phase of training. I was ready to go flying.

In contrast to the joyride I'd experienced as an NROTC midshipman at Pensacola, flying in an actual training squadron was a much more structured situation. The familiarization flights (FAMs) leading to your solo flight involved a student's personal instructor, known as the onwing. Mine was Lieutenant Jeff Nelson, one of the most demanding instructors in VT-27, a guy who helped give the squadron its reputation for being tough. He was known to be rough with lazy cadets and had no tolerance for those who didn't deliver their top performance.

After a particularly heavy afternoon thunderstorm, I showed up for FAM 1, my first flight with Lieutenant Nelson. In our brief meeting the day before, he had referred to a clipboard that listed my API and CPT scores, as well as my sixteen hours of instructed flight as a high school student in the Civil Air Patrol. Then he'd walked me out to the flight line, or tarmac, and went through a quick preflight walk-around on the T-34C that we were scheduled to fly the next day. He'd immediately begun throwing questions at me, pointing at the curved exhaust pipe and demanding to know the gas temperature or checking to see if I knew the proper inflation pressure of the tires. My answers had seemed to satisfy him.

The next morning he had me conduct the preflight

walk-around and explain every item I was checking. Once more, I seemed to pass muster. I climbed into the front cockpit, buckled my seat harness, and closed my canopy. Lieutenant Nelson immediately called for the before-start checklist, and I began to snap off the items, trying to keep up with his rapid questions.

After calling for taxi clearance, we joined the line of other Turbomentors on the long runway. Controlling the plane from the rear, Lieutenant Nelson ran up the engine for temperature, shaft horsepower, and rpm checks, and then got our takeoff clearance from the tower.

"Watch how it's done," he said into his helmet mike. "You'll be taking off tomorrow."

As on my first T-34C flight, the takeoff run was short and the climb-out smooth. We reached the training area above Padre Island at an altitude of precisely 5,000 feet. This wasn't like flying in the wide blue sky. There were other T-34C's around us, their young pilots learning the ropes just like me, and you had to be visually mindful of everything nearby. In fact, mindfulness, or situational awareness, is one of the main characteristics of a good pilot. You have to learn to focus on a number of things simultaneously, such as talking on a radio while studying your instruments and listening in your headset to what your copilot or navigator is telling you. Then you have to screen and process all this information and make the right decision as required by the circumstances. I don't know of too many professions that require this kind of multitasking for hours at a time.

"Give me a shallow three-sixty, five-degree bank angle, to the right," Lieutenant Nelson ordered.

I nervously eased the stick right while neither pushing forward nor pulling back so that the nose did not rise or fall. But I didn't succeed. Lieutenant Nelson's hand was on his stick, abruptly correcting my mistake: I'd let the right wing drop below 5 degrees and the nose dip. We had lost 50 feet of altitude.

"If you want to fly in the navy, Ensign," he said harshly, "you've got to do better than that."

He's going to give me a Down, I thought, angry with myself for my mistake. But Lieutenant Nelson was just probing to see if he could rattle me. Somehow I completed the turn and got back to our original heading at the proper altitude.

That night I studied the FAM 2 syllabus for hours. I had to memorize every detail of ground procedures and takeoff. The next morning I found myself in the aircraft with the engine throbbing as I checked my instruments a final time and advanced the throttle.

The plane howled down the runway as my eye jumped from the engine and airspeed instruments to the horizon. The rudder pedals came alive beneath my feet, and the plane just seemed to lift off by itself as we passed 100 knots. For the next few minutes I was actually flying, retracting flaps and talking to the tower for my departure heading all at the same time. Then Lieutenant Nelson took the controls and we went back out to the training area to practice other maneuvers.

After the landing, which he flew, Lieutenant Nelson told me to taxi back to the flight line and shut down the plane.

"Ensign, you didn't learn how to taxi an airplane like that in just sixteen hours with the Civil Air Patrol." His voice was grim.

"That's all the hours I have, sir."

Lying about this matter would be a breach of the honor code, a way to unfairly get ahead of my fellow cadets, something I would never consider. Lieutenant Nelson must have contacted a CAP officer back in Norfolk who verified my total flying time, because after that his attitude toward me softened somewhat. But he was still an exacting instructor.

Each FAM was intended to teach me something new about the T-34C and aviation in general. The sessions in the air were exhausting. As in ground school, I had to bring together everything I had learned before. On FAM 3, I landed the aircraft. Lieutenant Nelson noted that I had been about 5 knots too fast on touchdown, but he still gave me an Above for that part of the flight. The next day, however, I got my first Below Average when I blew a route-checking procedure. I was relieved to receive an Above Average for

Airwork that canceled the poor grade out, but was still disappointed in myself.

"Look, Ensign," Lieutenant Nelson said, "if you really want to do this, you need to get into the books and study what we brief."

Indeed, he had given me a small hand-drawn map of the training area the day before with the landmarks we'd be using in the morning. The mistake had been mine. You didn't get too many second chances with Lieutenant Jeff Nelson.

I was determined to do better, but for the next two weeks the weather turned nasty and my scheduled FAM kept getting scrubbed, or canceled. It was frustrating to study hard and then not be able to implement in flight what I'd learned.

This was how the FAMs went that summer. Each was a grueling physical and mental challenge, but somehow my skills did accumulate. I suppose this involved the equivalent of the visualization techniques that high-performance athletes use. Like them, I studied every aspect of the next day's problem intensely until I could actually picture myself performing the tasks.

Within a month, I was landing and taking off routinely and flying the crowded flight pattern around the field. But when I got too relaxed, the syllabus and Lieutenant Nelson would haul me up short.

We then began basic aerobatic maneuvers, which taught me, among other things, how to recover from a spin. This was serious stuff. In a spin, the airplane usually stalls and departs from controlled flight and basically becomes a falling object. From inside the cockpit, you look straight down and watch the earth twisting toward you in a sickening blur. If you can't get out of the spin or eject from the cockpit, you're dead.

As with everything else in primary, there was a procedure to deal with this emergency. Correctly coordinating ailerons, rudder, and elevators dampened the spin, but the maneuver had to be immediately followed by a three-G pullout. After Lieutenant Nelson demonstrated this a couple of times, he leveled off at 8,000 feet and said, "You try it now."

"Roger, sir," I replied uncertainly, and took the controls.

Once more my technique was not as pretty as it could have been, and I was a bit harsh on the pullout—my jaw sagged for a second or two from the G load—but Lieutenant Nelson conceded that it was a good effort.

Next we concentrated on basic instruments, the vital cockpit displays that told us the aircraft's attitude, its position in the sky relative to the earth. The gyroscope showed us if the wings were level and whether the nose was above or below the horizon, while the vertical speed indicator revealed how fast we were climbing or descending. It was one thing to practice with these instruments in a ground simulator but something else altogether to be sitting in the hooded rear cockpit deprived of outside reference points, banking, climbing, and turning while Lieutenant Nelson barked orders.

The weeks passed with the inevitable weather delays. By FAM 13, I had successfully learned how to deal with in-flight emergencies ranging from an engine fire or jammed landing gear to loss of power at high altitude. On the debrief after that flight, Lieutenant Nelson smiled. "You're going to solo tomorrow."

On the past several FAMs, I had been flying from the front seat, and my on-wing had kept his comments to a minimum. But I'd always been aware he was there behind me to take over in a real emergency. Now I was going to be on my own.

On August 23, 1997, I methodically worked through my preflight checklists and taxied to the end of the runway. I went to takeoff power and was wheels-up less than halfway down the runway. It was a hazy, humid Texas summer day, and I climbed into a nearly cloudless sky. With flaps retracted and power reduced, I continued the smooth ascent.

When I leveled off at 6,000 feet, I found myself grinning broadly. The navy had actually given me this fantastic airplane to fly, and they were paying me to do it!

I finished solo to the satisfaction of Lieutenant Nelson.

A few days later, I got called into the squadron office along with Ensign (ENS) Don Shank. From behind his desk, Lieutenant Nelson looked us both over before speaking up.

"You guys are doing the best of anyone in your class. You're natural aviators."

I was surprised. That was a real compliment coming from such a tough critic, but this wasn't just a confidence-building session. The squadron hadn't graduated enough students yet due to its own high standards and the bad summer weather. Lieutenant Nelson asked if Don and I would agree to accelerate our training, doubling up on our flights to complete over half the primary syllabus in just two and a half weeks. We said we would do whatever was best for the squadron.

We immediately moved into precision aerobatics, learning all the maneuvers that had evolved out of the elaborate airplane combat of World War I. I practiced all of these loops and rolls for hours, until I could string them together into a neat sequence. On my next solo, I flew out to the training area, swiveled my head around the sky to make certain nobody was nearby, and rolled the plane inverted. Hanging from my harness, I kept my right hand on the stick and used the left to snap a photo of myself with the earth and sky reversed outside the canopy. Of course, this wasn't an authorized navy procedure, but a lot of pilots did it, and I couldn't resist.

We finished primary by mastering the formation-flying curriculum (FORMs) in just three days. As partners, Don and I practiced exacting maneuvers that involved linked turns and breakaways in opposite directions followed by rendezvous on exact headings and altitudes. It was tough, rigorous work, but somehow I managed to study and prepare for each flight and transform that preparation into solid performance.

On September 30, 1997, I finished primary flight training at Corpus Christi. My total on the Naval Standard Scoring was fifty-five. You needed over fifty for jet training, and I had made the cut by a good margin. Once again, all the hard work had paid off.

But there was a problem. The navy's fleet of T-2C Buckeye jet trainers had been grounded for three months due to flight-control difficulties. This meant that there was a long backlog of candidate pilots waiting in the pipeline for T-2C training, and the navy wasn't accepting any more candidates.

I'd known for weeks that the jet pipeline was crowded, and had learned just how bad the situation was before I'd decided to accept Lieutenant Nelson's offer of accelerated training. If I had made up some excuse to delay completing primary early, I might have escaped the jammed T-2C pipeline and made it into jets later the next year. Instead, I had done what was best for the squadron.

Lieutenant Nelson told me to report to his office. I knew what was coming, and he didn't waste time getting to the point.

"I'm sorry, Shane," he said. "Jets just aren't there for you or Don. Both of you worked so hard for this."

I didn't know what to say. A future as a navy fighter pilot was suddenly closed to me. My dream was shattered. This was a huge setback, even more devastating than my car accident in high school and rejection from the naval academy. I kept thinking how unfair it all was. I had excelled in primary, yet it felt as though I was being punished for my success, all because of some inefficiency in the navy aviation pipeline.

When I calmed down that night, I told myself that life wasn't fair, and there were other options to consider. I thought about my mom's strength and the vets back in the VA home in Norfolk. I lived in the real world, and I had to accept it. All officers served to meet the needs of the navy. And the navy did not need any more fighter pilots at the moment.

I was twenty-three years old and had dreamed of flying since I was three. Now I had to get on with life and submit choices for other types of airplanes.

My first was the E-6A Mercury, a military version of the four-engine Boeing 707 that served as an airborne command post for our intercontinental missiles. Unfortunately, slots for the E-6A pipeline were also taken.

I didn't have any better luck with the C2-A Greyhound carrier-based turboprop plane. My final choice was the P-3C Orion maritime surveillance aircraft. It was a big, four-engine turboprop submarine hunter based on the old Lockheed Electra airframe. There were immediate openings.

Within a week of receiving the bad news about T-2C training, I got word that I would begin advanced training in November to enter the P-3C pipeline the next year.

My spirits rebounded. I would not be flying jets, but at least I would be flying. And I was determined to become one of the best P-3C pilots in the navy.

chapter eight

Before I could begin advanced training to qualify for the P-3C pipeline, I had a month to complete the requirements of intermediate training. In October 1997, under the supervision of Lieutenant Nelson, we began an almost daily series of long cross-country visual and instrument navigation flights, flying a T-34C all over Texas and points west. We even got in a nice aerial tour of the Grand Canyon. This was much less pressure than the training in primary, even thought there were lots of hours in the air. We managed to complete a three-month curriculum in just twelve days. Although I was tired, I understood more firmly than ever that when you train for the demanding profession of aviation, the more intensely you flew and studied, the better you became.

I moved on to advanced training with the VT-35 squadron, which was also based at the naval air station in Corpus Christi. There were only four students in our class, and we were the first to use the squadron's new twin-engine turboprop TC-12s, military trainer versions of a King Air 200, a conventional nine-seater commuter plane. With twelve aircraft to choose from, there would never be any maintenance problems to keep us from flying.

I was paired up with Ensign Kate Standifer as my plane mate. She was a natural pilot and a quick study. Our instructor was Lieutenant Don Hyde, a laid-back former pilot of a C-2A, a twin-prop commonly found on carriers to shuttle personnel back and forth.

Since we didn't have a simulator for the TC-12, we spent a lot of time in the actual cockpit, with Kate or me swapping into the left seat while Lieutenant Hyde flew. Kate and I developed a fun, friendly rivalry and pushed each other to do our best. The TC-12 is a two-engine aircraft, which meant we had twice as many engine instruments and controls to master as with the T-34C, and it employs a crew of only two. This requires a close-knit professional partnership between the two aviators, trusting the other to backstop you.

For example, one of the first big challenges was properly shutting down an engine in an emergency and continuing flight on a single engine. We practiced these procedures on the ground with our instructors until they felt we had enough knowledge and skill to be tested in the air.

In February, I went up with an instructor, Lieutenant Chris "Bucket" Burkett. I didn't know exactly when he was going to declare the "emergency," so I had to be prepared for anything. I was flying the takeoff from the left seat. It was nice, cool weather, and I got my clearance from the tower, turned onto the runway, and started the roll. Our wheels left the asphalt, and we were climbing to about 1,000 feet when I heard Lieutenant Burkett through my headset.

"Engine fire on number one."

Every sense I'd developed as a T-34C pilot warned me to leave that engine alone. Power meant lift; lift meant climb; climb meant life. But fire could kill you very quickly. I followed my briefed procedures.

"Emergency shutdown checklist," I said.

Lieutenant Burkett called out each item, and I responded, "Concur."

I kept the yoke at the same easy angle of climb and evenly pulled back the number one power lever to flight idle, to make up for the lost propeller torque with the rudder. I called to Lieutenant Burkett to raise the flaps, and then added, "Fire bottle number one." I hoped my voice was not too shaky. We continued to climb. "Feather number one." To feather an engine meant to shut it down so there was no power to the propeller.

Burkett's hands flew across the cockpit console. "Concur. Flaps up," he responded. "Concur. Simulated fire bottle." We weren't going to mess up a perfectly good tur-bine (engine) with real fire extinguisher chemicals.

I held the climb-out, simulating a call to the tower to declare an emergency. Although I had studied the aircraft manual, I guess I hadn't really been prepared for the fact that this aircraft could climb so well on a single engine. When we reached 2,500 feet, I leveled off and we restarted number one. Later that day, Kate flew the same emergency and did well.

That's the way the training went over the following months. Each week Kate and I learned some new, complex piece of airmanship. It was like building on a solid founda-tion. In the back of my mind, though, I was eager to move on to my real training in the P-3C and the discipline of mar-itime surveillance.

One day I mentioned this to Lieutenant Burkett. "You know, Shane," he said, "the EP-3E's missions are a lot more interesting than submarine-hunting in a P-3C. You might not get to bomb anybody or shoot any missiles, but you fly in some pretty interesting parts of the world."

I knew that the EP-3E ARIES II (Airborne Reconnais-sance Integrated Electronic System II) was a highly sophisti-cated intelligence-gathering aircraft and an integral part of naval air squadrons around the world. Chris had been with Fleet Air Reconnaissance Squadron VQ-1 when it had moved from Guam to Whidbey Island, off the coast of

Washington State, in 1994. He knew the airplane and the mission very well. He explained that the EP-3E was one of America's most capable platforms for collecting signals intelligence (SIGINT). With the plane's sensitive receivers and antennas, EP-3E crews could pinpoint a wide range of radar and radio emissions from enemies or potential enemies in international airspace. The crew was responsible for conveying that information to the ships and aircraft of the navy fleet, who could then develop an accurate picture of the electronic order of battle; this might include the electromagnetic activity of surface-to-air or surface-to-surface missile systems. The crew was also capable of providing direct real-time tactical electronic surveillance to U.S. fighters and strike aircraft, so they could better avoid threats and locate targets during combat operations.

The more he described his job to me, the more I wanted to go the VQ route. What made this choice especially attractive was that one of the EP-3E squadrons, VQ-2, was based at the naval air station in Rota, Spain, and staged missions over the Balkans out of Crete, one of the larger Greek islands. I had studied Spanish and liked the language. A three-year tour in Rota would be great.

First I had to type-qualify on the TC-12, a requirement for receiving my wings of gold. One evening in May, when we had about 150 hours flying time in the aircraft, Kate and I completed our solo night flights. We both passed the demanding hurdle. The final requirement would be the full-up check ride in which an instructor would put us through the wringer, testing every skill we'd learned.

As I approached this pivotal point, a crisis loomed in my personal life. In college, I'd been dating a girl named Jen, who attended school in Colorado. We'd become engaged when I was in flight school, and to be close, she moved to Corpus Christi. We were planning a big wedding in Colorado one week after I was scheduled to receive my wings, but the more I thought about getting married, the more I realized I wasn't ready. By definition, my life as a young navy pilot was going to be unstable. If I went the VQ route in EP-3Es, I would be on long detachments—what we called dets—away from my squadron's home base. That was not a good way to start a marriage. There was no way around the problem. The weekend before my final check ride, I sat down with Jen and told her my thoughts.

"I do not plan to get divorced," I said as honestly as I could. My parents' divorce was still unsettling to me, and I wanted my marriage to be as rock solid as possible.

At first Jen was stunned, but she understood my reasoning.

We spent the next day printing out and addressing don't-come-to-the-wedding requests to everyone on the invitation list.

One day later, I was sitting in the left seat of a TC-12, flying patterns above the Corpus Christi runway, as the instructor threw one order after another at me. When I banked left, I could look straight down at my apartment complex. There was Jen, loading suitcases into her car. She was moving out of my life. Although I'd known this was coming, I was still shocked.

I kept flying my check ride to the best of my ability. In the navy they taught us to compartmentalize our feelings. If you couldn't leave your problems at home, you shouldn't fly that day. Otherwise, you'd run the risk of killing yourself or somebody else.

On May 22, 1998, the moment I had been waiting for finally arrived: I received my wings of gold as a qualified navy pilot. I was one of the few ensigns that day to earn the honor, and I took great pride in the wings I now wore on the left side of my uniform and flight suit. Most of the officers around me had been in training long enough to have been promoted to lieutenant junior grade (LTjg). It had been exactly one year to the day that I flew my first FAM with the stern and unforgiving Lieutenant Jeff Nelson.

I was moving on the fast track again, and that was fine with me. I was ready and eager to begin my career as a naval aviator.

chapter nine

I was thrilled when I received my orders to report to VQ-2 in Rota, Spain, but first I had to complete P-3C training in Jacksonville, Florida. I had vacation coming, so I flew out to the naval air station in Oceana, near Norfolk, Virginia, to visit some old friends. Then I headed off cross-country alone on my new Harley-Davidson motorcycle, often leaving the interstate just to enjoy the country roads. It took four days to reach my dad's home in South Dakota. After a nice visit with my dad and his wife, Julie—my dad and I were getting along great now—I continued on to Nebraska to see my family there. I had worked hard for six years, and this was a well-earned vacation.

I reported to the naval air station in Jacksonville, Florida—Jax—to begin P-3C training in September 1998.

There I met several old friends from my NROTC days at the University of Nebraska and made a new friend named Paul Crawford. Paul and I discovered we shared the same birthday, the same political views, the same take-charge personality. We got along great.

The first morning we were introduced to the actual airplane, I began to understand that flying the P-3C and its EP-3E electronic reconnaissance variant would be as different as flying the TC-12 had been from the nine-seater T-34C. Everything about the P-3C was big. The wingspan was just under 100 feet, and the overall aircraft length was almost 105 feet. The tail stood as high as a three-story building.

The EP-3E was the same size but had its own unique profile. The Big Look radar dome, a bloated gray doughnut beneath the plane's forward belly, and a narrower canoe-shaped antenna cover farther aft, were both solidly attached. Smaller antennae were mounted beneath the wings and near the tail. All told, the EP-3E bulged and bristled with sensor pods, disrupting the original airframe's streamlined exterior and producing a lumpy appearance that some of my friends found ugly. But I've never seen a bad-looking airplane.

As the lieutenant instructor walked us around the hangar of the P-3C, rattling off statistics such as maximum gross takeoff weight (70 tons), I recognized this was an aircraft finely balanced between the power of its four big turboprop engines and the heavy payload of fuel and electronic equipment. The human factors of the twenty-four-member flight station crew also had to be finely balanced, with the workload spread among the rotating shifts of three pilots, two flight engineers, and a navigator.

In ground school, I entered a bewildering new realm of aviation. The course was taxing because the P-3C and EP-3E are some of the most systems-intensive aircraft in the American military inventory. A propeller engine, with its hydraulic, electrical, and de-icing systems, is far more complex than an airliner's fan jet. When you have an aircraft with four turboprop engines, that complexity is multiplied. The P-3C has miles of wiring and hydraulic plumbing, all controlled by a maze of circuit breakers, valves, and pumps. We had to memorize the function of every one of those systems and then begin the long process of learning what malfunctions could occur that lead to an in-flight emergency.

Although I had really stretched my brain becoming type-rated in the TC-12, I now had to cram in even more obscure knowledge. Flight engineers and instructor pilots taught us to spot the telltale signs of trouble in an engine by watching for brief, minor fluctuations in turbine inlet temperature and prop rpm. We learned to identify electrical overloads and to isolate the problem through a maze of circuit breakers. We spent day after day in parked aircraft or ground simulators, absorbing this blizzard of information.

While P-3C training at Jacksonville was intensive, much of it was spent on the ground. In fact, I got in only eleven training flights while I was there. But like the rest of my training, the flying was plenty demanding. By the third flight, I was able to fly a series of touch-and-go takeoffs and landings. This is a practice exercise where you take off moments after landing on the runway; it helps improve your landing skills. The next flight, the instructors began to incorporate emergency procedures for which we had trained in simulators. While flying at safe altitudes, I had to shut down a simulated overheating engine using the yellow-and-black striped emergency handle and then continue the simulation with the failure-to-feather procedure to prevent the runaway propeller from windmilling dangerously.

Many of the in-flight emergencies involved the engines. But we also had to deal with electrical failures that blacked out our radio navigation instruments, as well as hydraulic problems that forced us to manually release the landing gear.

Flap emergencies were some of the most demanding situations we had to deal with. The flap is the part of the wing that normally rotates up and down to help create either lift or drag, depending on whether you're taking off or landing. Every student pilot learns to handle fast, no-flap landings as part of the training curriculum for any aircraft. The bigger and heavier the airplane, the more critical this problem becomes. For the P-3C, normal touchdown airspeed with the flaps extended is around 120 knots (132 mph), depending on weight. The speed of a no-flap landing can be as high as 145 knots (nearly 160 mph). The plane has reinforced landing gear and can handle that speed. But those extra knots make a difference, and watching the runway go by you so fast takes getting used to. I've never been a timid pilot, nor have I been a "floater," using up half the runway to land. So I stuck my first no-flap landing right on the hash marks.

"I guess you don't believe in messing around," the instructor commented.

I took that as a compliment.

Just before I was scheduled to leave Jax in February 1999, my orders were changed from VQ-2 in Rota to VQ-1 on Whidbey Island. I was not a happy camper. Back in primary, I had accelerated my training to help my squadron and as a result lost my chance at the jet pipeline, despite the fact that I had jet grades. Then I had spent the next few months in a small class with a brand-new TC-12 curriculum with the understanding that I was earning my choice of assignment after P-3C training. Now, instead of going to sunny Spain, I would be heading to drizzly Puget Sound.

As usual, I calmed down after a while. I reminded myself I was in the navy and I had a duty to perform. I also knew that I would be in the same squadron as my good friend Paul Crawford and at the same base as two other friends, pilots Chris Rush and Greg Hodgsen. I was looking forward to serving with them despite the location.

As it turned out, there was another saving grace in getting my orders changed. About two weeks before leaving

Jax, I met a beautiful girl named Roxanne Faustino, whose parents were from the Philippines and whose father had retired from the U.S. Navy. It didn't take very long for me to realize this was a young woman I wanted to spend some time with. I left for VQ-1 feeling a lot better about being stationed in the States rather than overseas.

Before reporting to the squadron on Whidbey Island, I had to complete survival, evasion, resistance, and escape (SERE) school up in the mountains near Brunswick, Maine. I had come up through Scouting in Nebraska and had done my share of winter camping on the prairie, but February in Maine was like living in the Arctic. However, the instructors did teach us to survive. We dug sleeping caves in the snow, with a deeper central pit to collect the really cold air. We skinned rabbits and cooked them over smokeless fires of dry pine branches. We snowshoed across the bleak white mountains, following compass headings through the featureless pine and birch forests, evading possible capture. Each night as I lay shivering and hungry in my sleeping bag, I thought the same thing: I can't believe the navy's actually doing this to me. Even the marines who joined the aircrew in our class found the course tough.

One of the rougher parts of SERE was the prisoner-of-war exercise. The instructors were not as brutal as real enemy interrogators could be, but they were mean enough. Sleep deprivation was one of their favorite techniques. I hated going through the training, but I recognized its value.

I was an American military aviator who would soon be flying in harm's way. I had to face the prospect that I might be captured one day. After SERE training, I felt better prepared.

Still, I was glad to leave the frigid Maine woods. If I ever did have to parachute behind enemy lines, I hoped it was somewhere warm.

chapter ten

Not unexpectedly, Puget Sound was gloomy and overcast when I checked in for duty at VQ-1 in late April. Despite the weather, I thought the area was beautiful, especially when the mist lifted to reveal granite bluffs covered with dark green fir and spruce standing above the glittering water. Luckily, I was arriving just as the brief, sunny Pacific Northwest summer was beginning, and any sunlight highlighted the region's dramatic landscape.

VQ-1, the "World Watchers," was the navy's largest operational squadron, with about 75 officers and 350 enlisted personnel. The squadron always had aircraft and crews deployed to two permanent detachment sites. One was at Misawa on the Japanese island of Honshu (from which a plane staging out of Kadena Air Base on Okinawa flew). The other was in Bahrain, on the Arabian Gulf, to support Operation Southern Watch, the no-fly zone in southern Iraq.

Flying from the Western Pacific (WestPac) detachment sites, the squadron's EP-3E ARIES II plane covered the coast of Asia from the North Pacific all the way down to the South China Sea and, if required, into the Indian Ocean. To conduct our missions successfully, the EP-3E carried a crew of twenty-four, the largest of any U.S. military aircraft. Because our missions routinely lasted over ten hours, we carried three pilots and two flight engineers.

On checking in, I asked the assistant operations officer, LCDR Joe Sullivan, "When am I going to get a chance to go on the road?"

He looked at his status board. I hadn't qualified as a third pilot (3-P) yet. This was yet another specialized process that required passing two sessions in simulators, making three instructed flights, and taking a proficiency qualification standards (PQS) test about thirty pages long. An aircraft commander had to sign off on all qualification lines prior to the simulators and instructed flights. As in earlier training, I would be tested on all the aircraft's systems (turbines, propellers, and hydraulics) and the whole complex web of alloy, tubes, and cable that made the airplane fly.

"It looks like September," he said.

That was five months away. I tried not to show my disappointment.

"Can't I get out of here any sooner?"

He told me there was a detachment slated to depart for Bahrain in one month. The crew's 3-P had a pregnant wife and had requested to be excused from the det.

"How soon can you get qualified as a three-P, Osborn?" LCDR Sullivan asked.

"I think I can get qualified in a month, sir," I said, "if I can get the simulator and flying time in right away."

Sully looked at me skeptically; then he nodded. "Let's give it a shot."

Working furiously, I managed to get my qualification as a 3-P in time for the detachment. This was even tougher than accelerating through primary, but it was worth the effort. When the crew left for Bahrain, I was the 3-P.

Arriving at Manama in Bahrain was a shock. Our plane landed just after sunset, but the temperature was still about 115 degrees Fahrenheit. And this was not dry desert heat. The humidity of the surrounding gulf wrapped around you like a wet, salty blanket.

One of the problems with this weather was that the sand and humidity took its toll on the aircraft. Another was the extremely high temperatures; the plane's engine doesn't put out as much shaft horsepower in the heat. We had to fly shorter missions because we couldn't take off with a heavy fuel load for fear of losing an engine on takeoff and not being able to climb to a safe altitude. Somehow, Chief Wolcott and our maintenance staff gave us an up airplane for every mission. Working on the aircraft day and night under those conditions was brutal, but no one in maintenance ever complained, and we flew thirty-five straight missions without a maintenance cancellation.

Bahrain was the most Westernized of all the Islamic countries, and we were billeted, or housed, in some downtown luxury air-conditioned apartments. Our immediate group got along great, with officers and enlisted ranks treating each other as equals once we were off duty.

One of our jobs was to support Operation Southern Watch by flying a track within the borders of Kuwait, our ally. We were aware that Iraqi surface-to-air missiles didn't stop at borders, however, and that we presented a juicy target should Saddam Hussein, Iraq's leader, decide to become aggressive.

Because of the heavier fuel load required, we flew our longer reconnaissance patrols over the Arabian Gulf at night. One of our responsibilities was monitoring tankers, enforcing the oil export embargo the United Nations had imposed on Iraq. We also had to keep our profile of Iraqi forces up to date while ensuring the safety of the U.S. Navy carrier battle group operating in the gulf.

Early one morning in midsummer, we were just fifteen minutes from the end of a seven-hour mission, cruising at 24,000 feet and heading back toward Bahrain, when suddenly a yellow low-fuel-pressure light flashed on the fuel panel for engine number four. As 3-P, I was in the left seat, fighting off the fatigue of flying through the night, but I quickly came alert. We were about 140 miles from Bahrain and slowly descending.

Our aircraft commander (A/C), Ed Sung, suggested we continue on our normal approach. We would be landing in about twenty minutes.

"No, sir," Chief Dutrieux, the senior flight engineer (FE), said firmly as he looked from Ed to the instrument panel. "We're going home now."

"Roger that," Ed said.

Three minutes later, the engine lost about 2,000 shaft horsepower, almost half its performance.

"Emergency shutdown, number four," I requested

Petty Officer (PO) Wendy Westbrook, the FE undergoing training, stroked the number four emergency handle, and the outboard engine on the right wing immediately shut down with the prop neatly feathered.

About fifty miles out now, we got another low-fuel-pressure light, this one for the number two engine, and its shaft horsepower also began to drop. On the maintenance checks before takeoff, the ground crew had complained about finding some water in the fuel but were confident they'd fixed the problem by draining the bottom of the tanks. Now we all suspected the same critical situation: The fuel in our tanks was contaminated, either with water or something else, and our engines would flame out one by one until we became an uncontrollable 60-ton glider.

"Set condition five and prepare to ditch," Ed Sung announced on the PA. Condition five meant putting everything away, turning the seats around so that they faced the rear of the plane, and buckling yourself in for landing.

The plane was now being flown by our A/C and 2-P. I had moved to the back of the aircraft. Quickly, we all pulled on our helmets, hunkered down into our seats, and slipped on our harnesses.

Although we tried to keep our faces neutral, I could see that everybody was scared. All of my training had taught me how to prepare for an emergency, but I knew that no crew had ever ditched an EP-3E in the sea before. Everyone believed that the bulbous fiberglass radome of the Big Look radar protruding from the forward belly would plow into the water so hard, creating such instantaneous drag, that the plane would violently pitch forward on its nose—and the crew would be killed on impact. I thought about Roxanne, my girlfriend, and all of my loved ones.

Fortunately, luck was on our side that morning. We didn't have to test the chances of surviving a ditch. As the plane descended into warmer air, the power began to creep back up on engine number two. We made an uneventful landing with the number four prop still feathered. When the maintenance crews and safety inspectors investigated, they found the fuel tanks almost empty and a fair amount of water in each tank. The humidity had been so extreme on takeoff, they concluded, that we had actually carried our own water contamination with us to high altitude in the form of saturated air. As the tanks emptied, that humidity condensed into water, which sank beneath the lighter fuel and froze in the fuel lines, first starving number four, then number two. Only when we descended to warmer altitudes did the number two fuel line thaw out. Chief Dutrieux had saved our lives by calling for an immediate return to base.

If I ever needed a reinforcement of the advice all junior officers are given—"Listen to your chiefs. Rely on their judgment"—I got it that frightening morning over the Arabian Gulf.

chapter eleven

When I arrived back at Whidbey Island after my first det, my training pace slowed to a crawl. For the next four months, in fact, all aircraft were either deployed, grounded for modifications, or in need of repair for one maintenance problem or another. I was deeply frustrated. To qualify as a 2-P, the next step up for me, I had to fly a minimum number of training hops, spend time in a simulator, and pass a systems board exam with an instructor pilot. The test required you to have an in-depth knowledge of every working system on the plane, from hydraulics to electronics to mechanical. If you passed the exam, you almost felt like you were qualified to build your own plane.

I was finally able to escape from this limbo of

inactivity by taking my second det in January 2000, still as a 3-P. This was a WestPac detachment that began in Misawa and continued in Kadena on the Japanese island of Okinawa. There, the missions were much longer than we'd flown in the Middle East, and we were usually on our own, not working with an aircraft carrier battle group as we had in the Arabian Gulf. One of the best features about this det was that I could fly in a lot of different weather conditions, sharpening my skills.

In April, I returned to Whidbey Island and encountered an unusual opportunity. There was a det opening for a 2-P, and the squadron operations officer knew how badly I wanted to take it. However, to qualify as a 2-P, I needed nine more instructed flights and three simulator sessions, as well as a passing score on the systems board test. If the aircraft for the instructed flights and time in the simulators were available, the officer said I could take a shot at my 2-P.

"How much time do I have?" I asked.

"About two and a half weeks."

For every disappointment I'd experienced in the navy, I had come to realize there were an equal number of unexpected chances to advance myself, and this one was golden. I didn't want to blow it. Working day and night, I squeezed in all the required training. I sat for my 2-P systems board at six in the morning after a long instructed training flight that had ended at nine the night before. The board members threw one curve ball after another at me. I was exhausted, but I managed to pass. Unfortunately, I still needed my last check ride to be a qualified 2-P, and there just wasn't time.

Even though I was still a 3-P when I returned to the WestPac on my third det, my spirits were up. I knew it would only be a matter of time before I qualified as a 2-P. Another opportunity would somehow present itself, and I would grab it.

On my third det I was lucky to be with a terrific crew. My close friend Paul Crawford was the 2-P, and our EWAC (electronic warfare aircraft commander) was Lieutenant Norm Maxim, without question the best aircraft commander I've ever flown with. Norm was a tall, husky man with unruly red hair and a sarcastic sense of humor. A former enlisted man, Norm had a work ethic that wouldn't quit. He was one of the squadron's best instructor pilots and took it on himself to mentor Paul and me, a process that was far from easy.

The first day flying from Misawa, I was sitting in the right seat when he began peppering me with questions from the left seat.

"Let's say you experienced sudden but intermittent shaft horsepower drops on numbers two and three. Fuel flow looks normal. How do you proceed?"

I had no sooner answered that one than he shot back, "Split between the right and left gyros. Left displays alternating shallow banks. Right shows straight and level. It's a dark night. How do you determine which instrument is accurate?"

The questions kept piling up, and I did my best to answer.

Norm Maxim's relentless quest for excellence went beyond technical airmanship. He bombarded Paul and me with tactical questions from the mission commander's notebook. We were expected to learn the military structure and current geopolitical policies of all the nations in the regions that the squadron patrolled. This wasn't just some theoretical college seminar, but a practical requirement for becoming an EWAC and advancing to mission commander. At that level, an officer had to understand the exact nature of the potential enemy's military threat. If they painted your aircraft with fire-control radar, he asked, how likely were they to actually launch a missile? Naturally, we also were expected to stay as current as possible on our government's attitude toward these countries and understand the kind of intelligence we were collecting and the reasons it was needed.

"Hey, Shane," Norm said after my first exhausting quiz in the cockpit, "I'll help you study. You need to learn this stuff, and there's a lot of it."

"There sure is," I agreed, beginning to grasp the extent of the knowledge I needed to advance.

I accepted the challenge. Each night after flying, or

whenever our plane was down for maintenance, Paul and I headed over to the intelligence facility at Whidbey and began grinding through the hundreds of detailed files on the classified computers.

My efforts paid off. I qualified as a 2-P after I returned from WestPac in May. But Norm did not let up on me. Whenever he flew as my instructor pilot, he kept slamming me with increasingly tough questions.

"Don't forget, Shane," he'd always say, "the only way you'll make EWAC and mission commander is to study now. You don't want to wait until the last minute."

There was no disagreeing with him, and anyway, he wasn't the kind of person you argued with. He was bigger than life, and I respected him enough to spend almost every free minute at a classified computer in the Whidbey intelligence facility. A lot of people just kicked back a little and coasted between 3-P, 2-P, and EWAC. Normally, a pilot is expected to qualify as an EWAC two years after entering the squadron, provided there has been adequate training and deployment opportunity. I was determined, under Norm's prodding, to advance at a much faster pace, as I'd done with courses in the past.

That summer, I went on my second det to Bahrain. Norm Maxim was the EWAC, and Lieutenant Todd Lacy, the naval flight officer in charge of the back end, was the mission commander.

The heat was just as bad as on my first visit to

Bahrain, but this time the navy had billeted us inside its own secure compound, in poorly air-conditioned enlisted men's barracks, instead of the downtown luxury condos that I fondly remembered. The aircraft was in bad shape and required four engine changes in a month. I spent six or eight hours a day, every day, in the intelligence facility. If I wasn't studying, I was being quizzed by Norm and Todd. Knowing that I could already fly the airplane well, they concentrated on tactical and geopolitical knowledge.

Some of our quiz sessions got intense. They would hammer me with scenarios in which the aircraft received signals from extremely hazardous ground or air radars, indicating possible imminent missile attack. The degree of that threat depended on the political complexity of the potential enemy.

"What are his intentions now?" Todd would demand. He knew this stuff cold. I didn't. What was the difference in the political thinking of North Korea versus China? Russia versus Algeria? Iran versus Iraq? Who were the current leaders? Every country was different, every political agenda special, and they were always changing. I had to keep current.

"You have to make an immediate decision, Shane," Norm added. "When you're sitting in the seat, you don't have time to look up the answer."

I spent more time hunched over the computer screen.

Once again my hard work paid off. In September 2000, when I got back to Whidbey Island, I passed my EWAC board, seventeen months after reporting for duty to the squadron.

Then, still officially a 2-P, I left on my fourth det of the year, part of the first VQ-1 crew in Manta on the coast of Ecuador. Our mission was signals intelligence in support of the local antidrug effort. Lieutenant Junior Grade Jeffrey Vignery flew 3-P, our navigator was Lieutenant Junior Grade Regina Kauffman, and Lieutenant Junior Grade Johnny Comerford was the evaluator (EVAL), along with several other officers working with the "backenders," or operators in the rear of the plane.

Johnny was an extremely professional officer who had graduated from the U.S. Naval Academy at Annapolis in 1997 and been trained as a naval flight officer. He was one of the most squared-away EVALs I've ever worked with, not to mention one of my best friends. Jeff was a devoutly religious guy from Kansas with short, carrot-colored hair. Relatively new to the EP-3E, he was a good pilot who worked hard to learn our demanding profession. Regina had not yet officially qualified for her position; she had just joined the squadron and had a lot to learn.

It turned out to be a fascinating det. We were practically the only Americans in Manta. For most of us it was our first taste of the Third World, with the shocking contrast between the cramped shantytowns on the outskirts and the walled villas of the local elite inside the city.

Although some of the crew was saddened or repulsed by the widespread poverty, I saw things differently. The poverty was wrenching, but the people I mingled with in Manta relied heavily on their strong family bonds. Like the people I grew up with in South Dakota and Nebraska, they showed a lot of day-to-day courage and resourcefulness. They loved their children, worked hard, hoped for a better future, and endured.

We returned from South America just in time for Christmas. Needless to say, it was a shock to go from the humidity of the equator to drizzly Whidbey, then the whiteout blizzards of Nebraska.

As soon as my holiday leave ended, I was back at Whidbey Island, again studying hard. I had finished up my check ride for my electronic warfare aircraft commander designation prior to Christmas leave, but usually a pilot had to fly one det as an EWAC before qualifying as a mission commander. I hoped to get that det as soon as possible.

I was surprised and pleased in February 2001 when my squadron executive officer, Commander Michael Pagliarulo, called me in. He was the senior pilot in the squadron and was highly respected by all of the junior officers. "Lieutenant," he said, smiling, "you ready to take a det out to the WestPac in March?"

"Roger that, sir."

"Well, you've got it," he said. Then he grinned and extended his hand. "And you're going to go out as the mission commander."

chapter twelve

Settling in Japan wasn't any more difficult than getting used to Ecuador or Bahrain. My first month there we flew a dozen missions out of Kadena, making the routine nine- or ten-hour loop over the South China Sea.

The morning of April 1, 2001, started out just like any other mission. I stood on the tarmac at 0430 hours (4:30 A.M.), halfway through my inspection of the EP-3E ARIES II aircraft. Although the 3-P, Lieutenant Jeff Vignery, and my senior flight engineer, Senior Chief Nick Mellos, had already conducted their own rigorous walk-around inspections, the final inspection was my responsibility. As I ran my hand across the fiberglass skin of the forward weather radome in the nose, Senior (SR) Chief Mellos emerged from the shadows.

My first-grade picture.
I told everyone in school I was going
to be a pilot when I grew up.

At age ten with my mom,
my sister, Lynnette,
and my second dad,
Jerry Williams.

In my Civil Air Patrol
uniform at age thirteen
with my sister. I loved
being a member and
learning how to fly.

With Mrs. Monroe,
my favorite teacher at
Grant Elementary School.

I was the starting
wide receiver on
my high school's
football team.
Here I am at the
homecoming
game with my
dad, Doug, and
my mom, Diana.

Graduating from the
University of Nebraska
—on to the navy!

My Midshipman First Class cruise on the U.S.S. *Kitty Hawk.*

Practicing a parachute drag exercise during Aviation Preflight Indoctrination at the Naval Air Station in Pensacola, Florida.

My first flight instructor, Lieutenant Jeff Nelson.

At Primary Flight Training with a T-34C, the first aircraft I flew in the navy.

A Chinese F-8 II jet in flight.

Our damaged EP-3E plane at
Lingsui military airfield on the
Chinese island of Hainan.

Inspectors examine
the severed nose.

Grateful to arrive at Hickam Air Force Base in Hawaii with my crew after being held on Hainan Island for eleven days.

The awards ceremony at Andrews Air Force Base, where I received the Distinguished Flying Cross and the Meritorious Service Medal.

Returning a salute from Chairman of the Joint Chiefs of Staff General Henry H. Shelton as Secretary of Defense Donald H. Rumsfeld looks on.

Home at last! My whole family lined up to greet me at Whidbey Island Naval Air Station in Washington.

My EP-3E crew at Whidbey Island.
From left to right: LT Shane Osborn, LT Pat Honeck, SR Chief Nick Mellos, LTjg John Comerford, PO2 John Hanser, LTjg Jeff Vignery, PO2 Ramon Mercado, PO1 Shawn Coursen, PO2 Brad Funk, PO2 Rodney Young, LTjg Rick Payne, LTjg Regina Kauffman, SN Brad Borland, LT Marcia Sonon, ENS Rich Bensing, PO3 Steven Blocher, PO2 Ken Richter, AN Curtis Towne, PO2 Wendy Westbrook, SGT Mitchell Pray, SN Jeremy Crandall, PO2 David Cecka, and PO2 Scott Guidry.
Not Pictured: PO2 Joe Edmunds.

Honored to meet President Bush at the White House.

With his shaved head and graying mustache, Senior Mellos looked like a middle-aged pirate. But his green navy flight suit covered muscular shoulders and a barrel chest. He'd been in the navy for twenty-eight years, two more years than I'd been alive, and he'd spent most of that time flying on one variant or another of the P-3C Orion maritime patrol plane. We had known each other professionally and socially since Whidbey Island, and had flown a previous det to Japan together when I was a 3-P. I relied heavily on Senior Mellos's long experience as a flight engineer and leader to keep me up to speed on the condition of the complex airplane and the crew's morale. When he pronounced this aircraft "a solid airplane," with only minor maintenance problems, I felt certain we could make our takeoff time.

Using my flashlight, I inspected the nose wheel for tire wear and the shock-absorbing gear strut for leaking hydraulic fluid. I walked under the left wing and repeated the process with the main landing gear on that side, then peered up inside the dark wheel well to check the pressures in the two engine fire extinguisher bottles. Next, I stepped forward and reached up to grab the red-striped tips of the heavy gray alloy propeller blades of the number one and two engines, checking for obvious nicks or wobble. The four big engines could each produce 4,600 shaft horsepower. It was essential that the props be smooth and perfectly balanced or their runaway vibration could damage the aircraft.

On this det, the 2-P was Lieutenant Patrick Honeck,

with Jeff Vignery, the 3-P, flying his first det to the Western Pacific. Senior Chief Nick Mellos, with over eight thousand flying hours, was one of the most veteran flight engineers in the navy, and the other FE, Petty Officer Second Class (PO2) Wendy Westbrook, was a cool hand and a fast study. I knew from our experiences in Bahrain that I could trust her in the seat between the two pilots. As on our det to Ecuador, Lieutenant Junior Grade (LTjg) Regina Kauffman was our navigator, and Lieutenant Junior Grade Johnny Comerford was the senior evaluator (SEVAL) responsible for the eighteen surveillance personnel on board: cryptologic technicians, reconnaissance equipment specialists, and the special operators supervised by special evaluator Lieutenant Marcia Sonon.

The "backenders" all worked at in-line computerized consoles, which electronically gathered the intelligence that eventually got fed all the way up to the Pentagon. These highly sensitive computers and monitoring equipment were set along the sides of the back of the plane—the long, narrow tube that was broken up by the head (toilet), the small galley that looked like something out of a 1950s diner, and a stacked pair of curtained bunks for the off-duty pilot and FE, who could grab some sleep on long missions.

Adequate rest was a critical safety factor for our crew on a long mission, and we took turns grabbing some winks when we could. Even on autopilot, though, two pilots and one FE had to stay awake and alert for hours on end, because we flew visual flight rules—due regard. This meant that, unlike civilian airliners, we had to rely on ourselves, not ground controllers, for our safe separation from other aircraft.

I liked our entire crew—and their nicknames. I had tagged Johnny Comerford "Johnny Ballgame" after an old movie. Regina Kauffman was "Reggie." Pat Honeck was "Meeso." Nick Mellos was "Senior Mellos" or just "Senior," and Jeff Vignery was "Jefe." I was either "Sugar Shane" Osborn from my naturally sweet disposition (ha) or "Angry Osborn" when I was in a more demanding frame of mind. Jefe, Reggie, and Johnny had flown with me on missions in South America. Most of the others I'd gotten to know at Whidbey or around Kadena. We'd been together on this det about a dozen times.

I climbed the folding ladder to the main cabin entrance on the portside aft, and Senior Mellos secured the hatch. Now I was engulfed in the familiar scent of the airplane: warm electronics, a slight whiff of jet exhaust, and hot coffee in the insulated mugs some of the crew had carried on board. A few people looked sleepy. That day had been a "three-for-five," an 0300 briefing for an 0500 takeoff, which meant most of us had gotten up at 0200.

I assembled everyone in the cabin for a final plane-side brief. Even though we knew them well, I again reviewed procedures for ground and air emergencies, which might include the need to bail out or ditch the plane at sea. On entering the cabin, the crew members had taken a grease pencil and printed their names on their position line of the plastic ditching placard on the head door. Each line marked the number and storage rack of that position's parachute. Also stowed aboard the aircraft were our SV-2 survival vests and custom-fitted flight helmets. We all carried our own Nomex fire-resistant aviator gloves.

I completed the briefing on the ditching procedures by pointing to the two big life rafts stowed in the orange rubber soft packs near each overwing emergency exit hatch. Next, Johnny Comerford, the SEVAL, briefed the crew on bailout procedures. He was the jump master who would supervise the distribution of parachutes and make sure everyone got out of the plane correctly. Because the straps and harness on each parachute were preadjusted to fit a particular crew member, the chutes were carefully numbered.

We could all practically recite these instructions in our sleep, but this was a U.S. Navy aircraft on a demanding mission, and we followed the book in everything we did. In our case, that book was the *Naval Air Training and Operational Procedures Standardization* (NATOPS). Everything the flight crew did aboard the EP-3E was covered in that black three-ring binder thick with checklists, schematics of instrument layouts, and wiring diagrams.

After Johnny had reviewed bailout procedure in detail, I briefed the crew on the weather. "It looks like good weather en route to the track orbit and back to Kadena.

Excellent visibility and no reported turbulence at our assigned altitudes. Briefed mission time is just over nine hours today."

We were headed down the coast of Asia to the South China Sea. Once on track, we would fly our surveillance track in international airspace south of China's Hainan Island and north of the Philippines. Our squadron had been flying such missions in this area in one kind of aircraft or another for decades without serious incident. But we did expect that Chinese fighters would intercept us in international airspace at some point along our track. Once Chinese radar picked us up, their navy would usually dispatch a pair of twin-jet F-8 II Finback interceptors from the People's Liberation Army/Navy (PLAN) to look us over.

This harassment had been going on for years. Recently, however, the intercepts had become increasingly aggressive, not to mention dangerous. On January 24, for example, a Chinese pilot came within 30 feet of an EP-3E, hanging just off the American plane's left wing before he firewalled his throttles (sent the engines up to maximum power) and buffeted the EP-3E with jet wash in a crazy, dangerous maneuver called "thumping." Another pilot had flown close enough to another American reconnaissance plane to hold up a sheet of paper with his easily readable e-mail address.

This was reckless airmanship. The F-8 II Finback was a high-performance, air-superiority fighter capable of flying

Mach 2.2, or over twice the speed of sound, at almost 60,000 feet. The EP-3E flew much lower and slower, usually cruising at around 180 knots at an altitude between 22,000 and 24,000 feet. In order for a F-8 II to maneuver close alongside an EP-3E at that speed and altitude, the Chinese fighter had to fly dirty with flaps and slats extended from his thin delta wings, nose tilted awkwardly upward in what we call a high angle of attack (AOA). In this position, his plane was barely stable. Jet engines required a long spool-up (the time it takes from when you advance the power levers, adding gas, to when the engine actually starts putting out more power) to provide adequate thrust, and at these speeds, the pilot of a nose-high Finback needed a much greater throw of his stick to control the fighter's movements. That's called flying mushy.

These dangerous intercepts had prompted the United States government to raise a formal protest during the winter with the People's Republic of China. But it looked like the Chinese navy pilots flying the F-8s had not gotten the message, because we'd been intercepted even closer than that just the week before.

I'd been in the left seat, Jeff Vignery in the right. The familiar pair of Chinese F-8 II Finback fighters had appeared off the right side, as usual flying between us and their base at Lingsui on the island of Hainan. On some intercepts during this det, the Finbacks had given us a quick once-over, then dropped away and returned to their base; on others, they had stayed out there and hounded us for much longer. That morning, though, they'd seemed inclined to remain with us.

"They're co-altitude at three o'clock, closing," Jeff had said.

Straining forward in the left seat, I could see out the right-side cockpit window. There they were, two long, sleek gray jet fighters, their modified delta wings razor-thin and their towering, swept-back vertical tail stabilizers massive from this angle.

As we watched, incredibly, the fighters had slid even nearer to our right wing.

I'd alerted the crew to begin the standard intercept procedure. Observers had gone to their assigned windows, and Johnny had taken his clipboard to make detailed notes on the fighters' side numbers, ordnance, and behavior.

In the past, intercepts had usually lasted a couple of minutes, max. But on this day the Finback pilots had seemed determined to dog us. The lead fighter was mushing toward our right wingtip.

"Boy, they're close," Jeff had said.

"Meeso," I'd called Pat Honeck on the intercom, "come on up here to get some pictures." Pat had piloted S-3B Vikings off aircraft carriers and had a lot of experience with formation flying.

"Tell me how near they're getting," I had requested when he reached the flight station with his camera.

"He's probably fifty feet now," Pat had coolly announced, "maybe a couple of feet closer."

"Take some pictures of this guy," I'd requested. I wanted to have photographs showing the Finback's bright red side number as evidence of this reckless airmanship.

I could see the Chinese pilot's head distinctly through the streamlined dome of the fighter's canopy. His white helmet was emblazoned with a large red star on the brow, and his dark-tinted visor was down, touching the upper curve of his oxygen mask. None of his face was visible. I might have been looking at a doll pilot in a model—except that this was no model airplane. The Finback was huge right out there beside our wing. It was like looking out your living room window and seeing an elephant peering back in.

I had turned slowly away, easing off toward the north. For the next forty-five minutes, the two fighters had dogged us, one on our left wing, the other hovering right behind us, as if to make sure we stayed out of Chinese airspace.

To heck with them, I'd thought. We have every right to be out here. We're in international airspace, and I'm not going to let them push us off track.

But I kept my hands resting lightly on the yoke, ready to take over from the autopilot if it suddenly malfunctioned. When the Finbacks finally did head back toward their home base, my neck was knotted from the tension.

chapter thirteen

On this April Fools' Sunday, I finished my brief and made my way forward up the narrow center aisle toward the flight station. On the port side, Johnny Comerford's EWOPs were getting settled in at the consoles. Seaman (SN) Jeremy Crandall was stowing one of the binders of classified material Johnny had brought on board. Others along the line were plugging their headset cords into the intercom communications system (ICS) for voice checks before takeoff. The ICS allowed the crew to speak comfortably above the roar of the big engines.

Slightly forward on the starboard side, our navigator, Lieutenant Regina Kauffman, was hunched over the narrow chart table, plotting the first leg of our route southwest from Okinawa. Reggie was a small woman, maybe 5 feet in her stocking feet, and seemed to disappear into her seat. She was still a navigator trainee, so she had to be backed up on everything by the flight station. Senior Mellos was in the central flight engineer's seat, and Jeff Vignery, the 3-P, was in the copilot's seat on the right.

"What's up, Jefe?" I asked Jeff as I slid into my seat and buckled my harness.

"Senior says he's got us a strokin' airplane," Jeff replied, confirming Senior Mellos's initial evaluation that there were virtually no problems with the plane's complex maze of electronic, mechanical, and hydraulic systems. All the banks of switches and instruments on the flight deck gleamed. Taking advantage of the bad weather earlier in the week, our crew had cleaned the entire airplane inside and out, vacuuming, sweeping, and polishing. Even though the airframe had been built as a submarine-hunting P-3C Orion maritime patrol plane in 1969, five years before I'd been born, and there were the inevitable dents, chips, and scuffs visible throughout the cabin, this aircraft had always received excellent maintenance and had been completely overhauled in its conversion to an EP-3E. The process sometimes reminded me of the old Nebraska farm joke I'd heard back home: "This is my grandpa's axe. My dad changed the head, and I changed the handle."

I slid into my seat and buckled my harness. Speaking through our headset mikes, Jeff and I began the familiar challenge-and-response chant of the flight station checklists leading through engine start to final preparation for takeoff.

We patiently worked down the long checklist. One item was verifying that the two pilots' circular gyroscope artificial horizons were running. This instrument is divided between a black bottom representing the earth and a white upper hemisphere for the sky. The gyro displays our angle of turn and bank and the degree of climb and dive. The horizontal situation indicator (HSI) beside each pilot's gyro was an electronic compass that could be tuned to radio navigation beacons.

When Jeff and I were finished, I leaned toward the left windscreen and signaled the lineman below to remove the wheel chocks. Senior Mellos handed me a clipboard with the fuel quantity totals, center of gravity, and calculated takeoff speed. This was vital information. That day we carried 58,000 pounds—29 tons—of jet fuel. That would leave us the required minimum of 8,000 pounds remaining, or "on top," when we returned to Kadena after the nine-hour mission. If the field was closed for weather or any other reason, this reserve would guarantee us two hours to continue on to an alternative airfield in Japan.

The four powerful engines were started one at a time. Jeff and I had a count running; if any engine didn't start within sixty seconds, we'd have to shut it down. But the engine instrument panel showed the shaft horsepower, turbine inlet temperature (TIT), prop rpm, and fuel flow climbing steadily. Everything looked ready to go.

While Senior Mellos and Jeff finished up the final pretakeoff items on the checklist, I again studied the form with the fuel quantity, center of gravity, airfield temperature, and barometric pressure that comprised our takeoff speed information. Then I turned on my mike to speak to the crew in the cabin. "Set condition five," I ordered. Now everyone would turn and lock their seats facing aft and make sure their harnesses were secured for takeoff. A minute later, Johnny replied, "Condition five set."

After a final check of the instruments, I gave my take-off briefing to Jeff and Senior Mellos. On an EP-3E, engine performance is measured by turbine inlet temperature and shaft horsepower. The props are attached to a geared hub and automatically maintain 100 percent rpm, while the pitch varies with turbine speed. Because we were so heavy that day, we would need maximum continuous power.

"Okay, Senior," I recited in a quick, familiar sequence, "set ten-ten TIT on my command. Jeff, call out eighty knots for power and airspeed checks. We're looking for forty-six hundred shaft horsepower and we'll abort with less than forty-four hundred shaft on all four engines. Call out any malfunctions by type and engine number. We've got a good long runway, so there's no refusal today." By this I meant there was not a point before reaching rotation speed (the speed at which it's safe to pull the plane into the air) that we could no longer safely abort without running out of pavement if the engines weren't performing. "Call out rotate at a hundred and thirty-one knots. If we have a malfunction prior to rotate, I'll abort the takeoff. If we have a prop malfunction, I'll call for the appropriate E handle prior to bringing the power lever to flight idle."

The four yellow-and-black striped engine emergency handles occupied a prominent position at the top center of the main cockpit console. Pulling an E handle automatically shut down an engine both mechanically and electrically. Then the four propeller blades of the powerless engine would feather, locking in position so that their sharp edges faced directly into the airstream to minimize drag.

"If we have a malfunction after rotate at a hundred and thirty-one knots," I went on, intentionally repeating the rotation speed for emphasis, "then we're going to continue our assigned climb-out and handle the malfunction once we're safely airborne, in accordance with the NATOPS. Any questions?"

They had none. After a final round of checklist challenge-and-response items, Jeff and I turned our control yokes right and left, peering out our side windscreens to make sure the long ailerons on the wings' trailing edges rose and dipped properly. I pushed my control yoke forward and hauled back, and the lineman standing beneath my window signaled that the elevators in the tail's horizontal stabilizers moved freely. We were ready for taxi. The lineman snapped off a sharp navy salute, which I returned.

Jeff called the Kadena tower requesting permission to taxi to runway four left.

"Kilo Romeo nine-one-nine," the tower replied with our mission call sign, "clear to taxi."

Now the lineman was well clear of the left wing and the slashing propellers, signaling with lighted orange-cone taxi guides. I released the parking brake and eased the four power levers forward, my cupped right hand gripping their knobs. Given our weight that day, it took some engine thrust to overcome inertia and start us moving.

With my left hand I held the small alloy circle of the nose wheel steering system. We trundled down the wide taxi ramp, then made a turn. Swinging through the next turn on the taxi ramp, Jeff and I verified that the needles of our HSI compasses tracked from northwest toward north. We were almost at the end of the long ground checklist. Completing it day in and day out on either training or operational flights or in the simulator back at Whidbey was just one of the disciplines we accepted as naval aviators. You never took shortcuts in peacetime. Ever.

"IFF," Jeff said, referring to the radar transponder that squawked our aircraft identification for civilian ground controllers. We would switch this system from active to standby once we left Japanese airspace. "Set."

"Flaps," he said, repeating this vital checklist item. "Flaps set for takeoff." We both glanced down at the blue flap lever.

I eased the power levers back slightly, and the props whistled with the decreased pitch. Even though the taxi ramp was smooth, the big plane swayed, and the nose dipped with the change in speed. By now my eyes were well adjusted to the moonless night outside, so I dimmed the instrument panel a bit more as we reached the end of the runway.

"Harnesses," Jeff said, sounding off the last item on the checklist.

"Set," all three of us repeated, making sure the buckles were securely locked.

"Kadena tower," Jeff called, "Kilo Romeo nine-one-nine ready for takeoff."

"Kilo Romeo nine-one-nine," the tower answered, "take off four left. Wind oh-ten at eight. Cleared for takeoff."

We had 8 knots of wind, almost right down the pipe, which would give us a slight airspeed boost.

I moved the power levers forward again and tapped the top of the rudder pedals very lightly with my toes to test the brakes one last time. Even with this slight pressure, all three of us slid forward against our harnesses. The plane had very strong brakes, and they were tricky. You had to steer with the rudders on the takeoff roll, but if your toe accidentally touched a brake, you would blow a tire in a second.

Then you had to immediately pump the opposite rudder to overcome the swerve. If you were really unlucky and blew both tires on a main gear, you might not be able to keep the plane on the runway. You didn't want to dwell on what might happen if the plane spun off the runway at 100 knots, a landing gear collapsed, and the wing scraped along the pavement, sending up sparks. We carried most of our fuel load in wing tanks, close to the engines' hot turbines.

I had never suffered a blown tire on takeoff, but I had flown this malfunction score of times in simulators. It was an experience that always left me sweating, and it helped me learn early to respect the brakes. From our first days in flight station mock-ups, P-3C pilots were taught to steer with the balls of their feet on the rudder pedals, the heels of their flight boots resting on the deck.

I scanned the instruments again. "Everybody ready to go?"

"Roger," Senior and Jeff both replied.

Positioning the plane on the runway centerline, I slid the power levers forward. "Set ten-ten, Senior."

Senior Mellos continued to push the power levers full forward as I placed my feet on the rudder pedals and guided us down the centerline with the nose wheel steering. The plane gathered speed fast. My eyes jumped back and forth from the centerline to the lighted marker boards at the side of the runway to the airspeed indicator on the left of my instrument panel. At around 50 knots, I felt the rudder come alive through the soles of my boots, and took my hand off the nose wheel steering. Now I was holding the yoke forward to keep the nose down and prevent bouncing as we accelerated. Pumping my feet smoothly, I kept us centered on the runway.

About ten seconds after I had begun steering with the rudder, Jeff called out, "Eighty knots."

We both scanned our airspeed indicators to make sure there were no splits, that we were registering the same. Mine indicated 80 knots and rising. The boards were flashing by now. We also scanned our engine gauges for malfunctions. There were none. The engines roared with solid power.

Soon we were passing 131 knots, and Jeff called out "rotate." I smoothly and cautiously lifted the aircraft off the deck. "Positive rate of climb," I said. "Gear up."

Jeff's hand was already reaching for the tire-shaped end knob of the lever. "Gear up," he replied, adding a moment later, "Locked." The nose and main gear came rumbling up and folded into their wells with a comforting thump.

As we cleared the runway and the plane lifted into the clear, starry night, I watched the airspeed closely. We were quickly approaching 160 knots. The maximum speed for takeoff flaps is 190. But I didn't want to retract the flaps to the maneuver position a moment too soon because we needed every bit of extra lift they gave us. I also didn't want to go too fast with the flaps extended, as that might damage them.

Just above 160 knots, I told Jeff, "Flaps to maneuver."

Senior Mellos reported the cabin was pressurizing normally as we climbed, and the prop synchronization was on the money. Approaching 180 knots, I called to Jeff to retract the flaps.

"Speed checks," he read from his checklist, "flaps coming up."

Again, both our airspeed indicators matched and the flaps had retracted completely. It looked like everything was running smoothly. Climbing through 6,000 feet, we left the long, narrow island of Okinawa behind us and rose into the dome of stars above the dark Pacific.

Japanese air traffic control cleared us for a climb to a cruise altitude of 18,000 feet in slow, 2,000-foot increments. This gave us time to burn off some fuel and speed up as we became lighter. Before the people in back could undo their harnesses and swivel their seats back around, I called, "Set condition four." A crewman then got up, put his helmet on, and went to a side window to check the engines for smoke and inspect the nooks and crannies where hydraulic lines and pumps were hidden, looking for leaks. There were no problems to report.

"Set conditions two and three," I called over my mike. This meant that the crew would finish preparing their equipment and that all systems were go. Now the crew could finish preparing their equipment or just relax as we droned south. Although I had flown hundreds of takeoffs during my five years with the navy, I still found this demanding, disciplined process completely satisfying. April Fools' Day or not, it was a great morning to fly.

chapter fourteen

By 0625 Okinawa time, almost ninety minutes after takeoff, we were at 21,500 feet, heading toward the Luzon Strait between the Philippines and Taiwan. Because the EP-3E had so many external antennas, our airspeed was restricted to 250 knots unless there was an emergency. That day we droned along on autopilot at the usual 210 knots during our cruise to the track line. Once on track, we would slow to 180 knots to conserve fuel.

As forecast, the morning was beautiful and clear, with just a few broken clouds far below. Petty Officer Wendy Westbrook came up to swap out with Senior Mellos in the flight engineer's seat so he could get some rest.

After fifteen minutes of chatting with Wendy and Jeff, I decided that sleep sounded pretty good. Jeff could fly the airplane from the left seat, and Pat Honeck could sit in the right. Out of habit, I held the overhead grab rail as I made my way aft through the cabin, even though there was no turbulence. Some of the crew were still loading software in their equipment, while a few people thumbed through training manuals and magazines in the galley.

Stretching out in the upper rack, sleep did not come easily. I've always been a light sleeper, and an EP-3E rumbling along toward its track orbit was not exactly a restful environment. After I pulled the curtain tight around the bunk to shield my eyes from the high-altitude sunlight, I scrunched up the pillow and readjusted my foam rubber earplugs. But half my mind was still listening for any change in the engine noise and bracing for an unanticipated bank or turn.

As mission commander, you can never totally relax. You never know when trouble will come knocking at your door.

I had not been able to sleep in the curtained upper berth. Finally, at 0800 hours, I dropped down to the deck and pulled on my life preserver unit, still feeling a little groggy. By the return leg of the mission that afternoon, I figured I would be tired enough to sleep deeply. Now I had to relieve Jeff in the flight station.

Passing the galley, I grabbed a bottle of water, took a long swig, and moved forward up the center aisle of the tube. I stopped at Johnny Comerford's position, number thirteen, to review some details of the day's mission, which we'd been briefed on before takeoff in the intelligence facility at Kadena.

"How's the gear working?" I asked, leaning close to his head to be heard above the engine noise.

"The back end's looking good, Shane," Johnny reported, indicating that our reconnaissance equipment had been tested and was functioning well. He had our track line plotted on a laptop computer. "We'll be on track in about twenty-four minutes."

In addition to being a good friend, Johnny was also one of the smartest people I'd ever met, quietly confident and rigidly self-disciplined. His job was demanding, and he always rose to that challenge. I was grateful to have him on my crew.

Passing the nav station, I saw that Regina was again carefully updating the navigation systems by downloading into them the latest GPS (global positioning satellite) position, which also gave us our ground speed. By keeping our position current, we would arrive at the start of the track line at the exact place and time we'd briefed back at Kadena.

On that day's track, we would fly an irregular box pattern over the South China Sea that kept us well within international airspace. To a nonaviator, that kind of navigation might have seemed tricky, but we had been doing it so long that it was second nature. It was all just a question of confirming our position by GPS and our navigation systems as we went onto the track heading, and then making the correct turns onto new headings at the required times, reconfirming our position each time we did so. This was like driving along invisible highways in the sky, making sure we stayed in our proper lane. While commercial airlines and civilian jets, guided by air traffic controllers, flew at even-number altitudes, we flew at odd-number altitudes. This was to avoid any possible midair collision.

That day our track altitude was 22,500 feet, and that's the altitude we'd reached when I swapped out for Jeff in the left seat. The morning was bright and crisp, a sign that a high-pressure weather system dominated the area. Our gauges showed that the outside air temperature hovered around 8°C (around 46°F).

After buckling my harness, I took the control yoke and switched off the autopilot with my right index finger. "I've got the controls," I said into my headset mike, formally announcing that I was flying. I wanted to get the feel of the plane's trim and balance before we went back on autopilot and got on track. Unlike many large planes, the EP-3E is inherently unstable and takes constant fine adjustment with the controls to fly straight and level. For that reason, we relied on the autopilot to keep the plane stable during the long patrol flights.

We were still fuel heavy, and I saw that Pat and Jeff had used the autopilot to rotate the wheel of the elevator trim tab a few degrees forward to help keep the nose level with the horizon. The trim tabs are small movable panels on the elevators, ailerons, and rudder that we could adjust without continually using the control yoke or rudder pedals. Later, when we burned off even more fuel, we could ease some of the nose-down trim.

When I switched back to autopilot, the plane settled into a solid groove. "Nice and smooth, Meeso," I said.

"Nice to have a machine to do the work," Pat replied.

Wendy Westbrook handed me a form that she'd just completed. "The fuel numbers, sir."

Even though I knew her fuel calculations would exactly match the quantity gauges on the center console, I double-checked her work, comparing the numbers with the gauges. In the navy, we followed procedure.

"Looks good," I said, handing back the form.

Any flight engineer mentored by Senior Chief Nick Mellos was certain to do things right. This was how naval aviation worked. Our squadron trained constantly, on simulators, on spare P-3C Orions (which had the same flight station as the EP-3E), and during dets. This was what discipline meant.

As we droned southwest through the morning, I thought about the years of discipline that had gone into my own training, and felt comfortable that I was prepared for any situation.

chapter fifteen

About 0830 hours, sitting in the pilot's chair, I banked the plane right to the track, exactly on schedule. The sky was still cloudless, the ride smooth. I eased the four power levers with my right hand and watched the shaft horsepower and TIT drop evenly on the engines. Wendy Westbrook reached up to adjust prop synchronization and minimize vibration.

"A hundred and eighty knots on the nose, Shane," Pat Honeck announced.

My airspeed indicator matched his. "Roger that, Meeso."

Regina Kauffman checked in to report that our heading to the first turning point was "right on the money."

I held the control yoke firmly to verify for myself

that we were on the correct heading, at the briefed altitude of 22,500 feet. Everything looked good, so I reengaged the autopilot, and the plane settled solidly on track. Then I flipped my mike to the loop that connected directly to Johnny Comerford.

"Hey, Ballgame, what's the situation back there?"

"Shane, systems are up and running. We're getting some activity back here."

By that he meant the plane's powerful sensors were already picking up interesting electronic data from a variety of sources, and that our in-line operators were analyzing some of these signals. The business of intercepting and analyzing data was a highly technical specialty, and while I didn't know much about it, it was important to me that Johnny and his group got what they needed. This was why we flew these missions.

My eye went to the fuel gauges on the center console. We were in good shape and could extend our track time if there was a good operational reason, as long as the weather en route back to Kadena did not deteriorate.

My stomach growled. It had been over six hours since I'd eaten a breakfast bar and gulped a little carton of OJ back at Kadena. Turning the controls over to Jeff Vignery, I fetched another bottle of water from the galley and worked my way forward, chatting with the cryptologic technicians and electronic warfare operators at their positions. Then I paused at Johnny's station.

"So far this is a textbook mission," he said.

"Except for no intercept," I replied, referring to the Chinese pilots in their sleek gray jets.

He nodded. "Well, as the man said, it ain't over till it's over."

I hoped he was wrong. The previous week's intercept had been a nasty experience.

I returned to the flight station and swapped out for Pat Honeck in the right seat. Wendy Westbrook had taken over for Senior Mellos, who was back in the galley, preparing rice in the electric cooker. I pulled on my headset, studied the instrument panel, and listened to the crew's professional exchanges. We were now on the long final leg of the day's track, heading southwest away from the Asian coast. Reggie checked in over the intercom with a position update. Currently, we were 70 nautical miles south-southeast of Hainan Island.

"We've got about ten more minutes on track before we need to head home to make land time," I told Jeff and Wendy.

By now it was exactly 0955 hours Okinawa time. Our current estimated time of arrival (ETA) back at Kadena was 1356 hours, giving us a mission of slightly less than the nine hours we'd briefed. Even the winds had been favorable that day.

As we lumbered through the tropic sky, the sun climbed higher and swung in front of us. Both Jeff and I adjusted our green plastic windscreen sun visors. Jeff also cleaned and replaced his pilot's sunglasses. I never wore glasses of any kind because I couldn't stand to have anything near my eyes after the car accident in high school.

Scanning out the right cockpit window, I suddenly saw a familiar pair of Chinese navy F-8 II Finback fighters about a half a mile out, climbing to our altitude. The People's Liberation Army/Navy had not forgotten us after all.

From the right seat, my view was much better than it had been during the previous intercept. The fighters were still in loose trail formation, but the lead pilot had misjudged the relative speeds and overshot us by a good quarter mile. He had to haul back on his stick to bleed off airspeed by jerking the dark, bullet-shaped nose of the Finback into a high angle of attack. That was the kind of sloppy maneuver that would have earned you a Down from Lieutenant Jeff Nelson in primary, I thought.

Fortunately, the Finbacks were far enough away to not cause us concern. Once more I alerted the crew, and the observers took their stations at windows.

"Three o'clock, level," the starboard aft observer reported. "Their trail is about two hundred feet lower than the lead."

So far, the fighters had shown no sign of closing the gap.

"I've got the controls," I told Jefe, beginning a shallow 5-degree bank away from the fighters, and using the autopilot for the gradual turn. I had no doubt they would follow their typical pattern and stay on the island side, shadowing us before falling back to return to Hainan while we moved on to our northeast heading toward Okinawa.

If we hadn't been at the end of our mission, I would have completed the turn back and continued to fly the track line.

Now something strange happened. The port aft observer checked in. "I've got the two fighters at about our seven o'clock position low, and they're closing."

Instead of drifting back to return to Hainan, the Finbacks had shifted their position to our left side and were approaching from the rear.

"They'll probably just take a little look at us," I reassured the crew. "Then they'll peel off to go home themselves because we're headed away from them."

Holding the shallow bank with the autopilot, I watched my compass swing slowly to 070, northeast, our homebound heading. The autopilot had kept the plane rock solid the entire time, but once more, with fighters nearby, I rested my hands on the yoke, ready to take control if necessary. Pat Honeck and Senior Mellos had come up to stand behind us in the flight station.

The observers on the portside kept up a steady stream of reports. Lieutenant Marcia Sonon, the special evaluator, was crouching beside Johnny Comerford at the little round window of the portside overwing hatch. "He's closing to three o'clock," she said, her tone flat and professional. "He's definitely armed. I can see missiles on his wings."

Suddenly her voice grew tense. "He's getting really close. Fifty feet. Now he's about forty feet. Oh, my God, he's coming closer. Right now he's about ten feet off our wing. He's making some kind of hand gesture to us, but I don't understand what he's trying to do."

Jeff and I exchanged an alarmed glance. From the right seat, I could not see the Chinese pilot's gesture, but Marcia was a trained observer and would not exaggerate.

I eased the four power levers slightly forward to increase our airspeed to 190 knots. I didn't want that guy going into a stall this close to our wing. The Finback II had a landing speed of 156 knots at sea level, so it was amazing the pilot could stay even with us in this thin air. All we could do was monitor the autopilot and sweat it out.

In fact, I was starting to sweat a lot. My T-shirt beneath the open collar of my flight suit was already damp, despite the fact I had my air-conditioning vent cranked up high.

Pat leaned toward the left-side cockpit window. "He's not very stable out there, Shane, and he's getting very close."

"Yeah. He's close, really close," Jeff confirmed, looking scared. I know I must have too.

"I'm already turned away," I snapped. Then I added

in a more even tone to ease the tension a little, "There's no place for me to go."

Just to reassure myself, I studied the HIS compass. Our heading was an unwavering 070 degrees.

"Okay, he's dropping off some," Jeff announced. The relief in his voice was obvious.

"Now he's back toward our seven or eight o'clock position," Marcia confirmed.

That had been a bizarre, and frightening, experience. Where had that guy wanted us to go? We were in international airspace, turned away from China, and I couldn't maneuver the huge aircraft with him so close. All at once I had a weird thought: This is going to be a long mission report. I would have to write up the dangerous intercept in detail because the Chinese pilot came so close and acted so aggressively, even while we were headed home. I knew my report was bound to create a lot of concern in the chain of command.

At least the intercept had ended. We were going home.

My peace of mind lasted for all of thirty seconds.

"Port aft," one of our observers reported. "Here he comes again. He's closing, he's closing fast."

Pat was still at his window. "Yikes," he gasped. "He almost hit us."

I felt a flood of adrenaline, simultaneously icy and hot. "What do you mean?"

Pat pointed wordlessly. The fighter's fuselage was just below our wing, but our two cockpits were side by side at the same level. Even from the right seat, I could see the fighter's nose was drifting in front of and inside the span of the left wing, only feet from the slashing disks of the four-bladed propellers. Now the Chinese pilot had dropped his oxygen mask. We were eye to eye and he was mouthing silent, angry words, gesturing at us with his open gloved hand as if trying to wave us away.

I was gripped by dread. How could he try to fly his plane with one hand in these conditions? The only way the pilot could control the Finback effectively was with one hand on the throttles, the other on the stick—and he wasn't doing much of a job of it, because his nose was chopping up and down.

There was nothing I could do. It would be too dangerous to try to maneuver with him flying so unstably just beneath our wingtip.

Then, as quickly as he had come, the Chinese pilot dropped away again. I released a breath. This definitely was going to be a long report.

Suddenly Pat shouted, "Here he comes again! He's closing really fast this time."

What is this guy doing? I wondered again. I was furious with him for his recklessness, and at the same time scared to death.

Pat was suddenly yelling, his words loud and indistinct. But I saw where he was looking. There was a fractured blur at the left wing. The Finback had approached again from our left rear, closing so fast the pilot couldn't slow. Instead of dipping his nose to fly beneath our wing, he pitched up and tried to turn away to stop his rate of closure. But it was too late. He was already inside our wing. And when his nose shot up, the fighter's long fuselage rose at a steep angle toward the chopping propeller blades of our number one engine.

"God . . . ," Pat shouted.

The rest of his words disappeared in a blast of noise. A harsh, abrasive chattering filled the cockpit, as if we were speeding down a stretch of terrible washboard farm road. I saw a cloud of glittering debris blowing out in front of our left wing. The sickening chopping continued, sounding like a monster chainsaw hacking metal. My hands gripped the control yoke tightly, and I felt each jarring impact.

The unimaginable had happened. The pilot had just smashed his plane into ours.

chapter sixteen

Inside the plane, people were shouting in fear and disbelief. I realized that the propeller of my number one engine had struck the fighter jet where its vertical stabilizer joined the fuselage. It had cut the Finback in two. That's what the chainsaw chopping noise was.

Now, as that noise ended, a thick, dark shape—the front section of the Finback—flipped toward us. It was like trying to get out of the way of a falling meteorite with nowhere to go.

The front half of the Finback smashed directly into our nose.

The impact blasted like an exploding missile. Another huge, dark shape—our own severed fiberglass nose cone—whipped up and over the windscreen and disappeared into space. Everyone in the flight station yelled and cringed.

The first blast was instantly followed by the clap of explosive decompression and the unshielded roar of the engines as the forward pressure bulkhead was punctured. Freezing air was now streaming in at us with incredible force.

I shuddered to see the Finback's severed fuselage— the back half—falling beneath our plane. It had narrowly missed the right wing and the propellers of engines three and four.

People were still screaming around me as our noseless plane pitched up, the left wing dropped violently, and we snap-rolled steeply left. It was almost impossible to think with the entire plane chattering and shaking so violently from the damaged propeller and the rush of air through what once had been the plane's nose. But I had to stay calm and remember all of my training.

I immediately realized we were going into an inverted dive. That was a flight attitude even the EP-3E's robust airframe couldn't endure. Instinctively, I swung the yoke hard right and jammed my foot on the right rudder pedal. The plane kept rolling left and the nose kept dropping like a stone. I caught a glimpse of the gyro on my instrument panel. The black-and-white hemispheres were supposed to be horizontal. Instead, they were vertical. We were swinging past a 90-degree bank angle, headed toward inverted flight. I knew from my training in primary, specifically the aerobatic maneuvering, that an inverted dive was fatal.

This guy just killed us, a voice sounded in my head as I fought the controls. The air was streaming through the flight station as our speed increased.

"Get control of it!" I heard Senior Mellos bellow hoarsely from somewhere behind me. "Get control of it!"

I had the yoke turned vertical, full right, and my boot was jammed down on the right rudder pedal. But still we rolled left and the dive angle grew steeper.

I was now looking up at the soft blue plain of the South China Sea. Through my right overhead window, I saw the forward half of the Finback's fuselage continue to drop beneath us with flames and black smoke spewing out.

What looked like a grayish-white parachute drifted away. Had the pilot had gotten out alive? I wondered. I felt weirdly detached from the scene, as if I were watching grainy old Vietnam War footage on television. Then I realized our plane was falling at almost the same speed as the crippled Finback's burning wreckage. We were not flying. We were dropping out of the sky.

We're going to die, I thought again, still battling the controls. This is the worst nightmare I've ever had, only it's real. We're still high in the sky. This plane won't fly. We're all dead, and it's going to take a while for us to hit the water.

I kept wanting to get over that thought, to do

something, but the shock was severe. As our dive angle increased, so did our airspeed. The airstream was shrieking through the holes in the pressure bulkhead. Unless I managed to roll us back wings level and raise the nose, we would continue rolling into full inversion, the nose would drop to vertical, and we'd be in a spin from which no four-engine aircraft could ever recover. Already, I saw that our bank angle was around 130 degrees and the nose had dropped 50 degrees below the horizon.

I could not just give up and surrender to the inevitable. I was responsible for twenty-three other crew members. The navy had trained me for five years to confront any and all emergencies. I would continue to fight as long as I could.

Logical thought began slowly to overcome my shock. Okay, part of my mind told me, we're snapping hard left, nose way down. Keep full right aileron and rudder. You've got to stop the roll rate. You can't let it get all the way inverted.

But take it easy on the pitch pullback, I reminded myself. From the vertical speed indicator, which was pegged out at its maximum rate of 6,000 feet a minute, I saw we were dropping far faster that the airframe's design limit. This horrible dive was also taking us into thicker air. The combination of airspeed and air density might produce enough flow over the ailerons to let me bring the wings level before our airframe was torn apart. I couldn't haul back on the control yoke to pull us out of this dive until I did have the wings level, otherwise I'd overstress the tail for sure—then we'd definitely lose the elevators. That too would be fatal.

My mouth was cotton-dry from the explosive decompression and the adrenaline pumping through my body. I looked down at my hands. The control yoke was almost impossible to hold steady because of the intense buffeting. The incredible vibration, I figured, meant that the number one prop located furthest out on the left wing had been damaged in the collision. Our four props were meant to be as finely balanced and synchronized as clockwork. Even the slightest misalignment meant that a pilot would feel something in the yoke. And what I was feeling now—worse than anything I had ever experienced in a simulator—told me that the damage to the plane might be beyond recovery.

What if not just the props but the hubs holding the props had been damaged? What if the gears, inside the hubs, had been stripped, and the prop flew off? My nose had been hit; if my hydraulic line located on the nose wheel had been severed, I could never move the ailerons on the wing or the elevator and rudder on the tail—I would have no control in landing.

I tried to push away those thoughts and ignore every discomfort as I held the yoke hard right, gazing out the windscreen at the vast blue sea above.

Somehow I had to get this plane turned right side up.

chapter seventeen

As I kept pushing the yoke hard right, very slowly the blue field began to move from above me to the right of me. The plane was so big and lumbering that even under normal circumstances it didn't turn on a dime. Now it felt more like I was trying to fly an oil supertanker in the sky. I kept my eyes outside the cockpit, following the painstaking aerobatic instructions I had received a couple of years before from Lieutenant Jeff Nelson at Corpus Christi. I could almost hear Lieutenant Nelson's stern, confident voice. "If you've got daylight," he'd told me, "get your head outside the cockpit to judge your attitude." It was a lesson no good pilot ever forgets.

I put my entire head outside the cockpit. There was no doubt now that the wings were gradually rolling level, even as the airspeed increased far beyond the hazardous maximum. However, I had no way to judge this because my airspeed indicator was actually slowing. It was probably broken, but I'd worry about that later. For the moment, it was critical that I recover from this roll.

Just as the airstream from the broken nose through the flight station had risen to a shrill, deafening howl, the face of ocean below us stopped moving right. My eye shot to the gyro. The two hemispheres had again reversed, with white above, black below. That meant the wings were level, but we were still nose down, dropping fast to about 15,000 feet. The collision had occurred at 22,500 feet, which meant we had fallen almost 8,000 feet in about thirty seconds.

Again, I tried to think as I'd been trained for all emergencies: in a precise and logical sequence. But that was hard because the plane wasn't behaving in a precise and logical manner. I realized I was only able to keep my wings level if I had the yoke vertical, full right, and my foot down hard on the rudder pedal. But the sickening vibration and shudder of the number one prop threatened to shake the wing apart. Worse, I saw that the propeller was still spinning at 60 percent rpm. If we didn't get that engine shut down immediately, one of the chewed-up blades could fly off the shaft hub and rip into the fuselage just behind the communications station, cutting control cables and hydraulic lines—another fatal scenario.

I faced Wendy Westbrook in the engineer's seat. "E

handle number one," I yelled, instructing her to shut the engine down both mechanically and electrically. Wendy seemed dazed. I took a chance and removed my left hand from the top of the yoke just long enough to reach over and grab the number one E handle. "E handle one," I repeated, shouting even louder.

Senior Mellos and Pat Honeck were back on their feet. During the snap roll and near inverted dive, the plane had remained under positive G forces. People had been pressed against the deck but not tossed to the overhead. Senior tapped Wendy's arm, and I knew they would get that engine shut down.

All I had to do then was pull us out of this dive, but the truth was, I wasn't sure I could. In thirty seconds we had fallen 8,000 feet and were gaining speed. In another thirty seconds, our altitude might be as low as 5,000 feet . . . and then it would be too late to do anything.

With my right thumb on the yoke, I flipped from the normal intercom to the PA mode. "Prepare to bail out," I ordered.

I turned to Jeff Vignery. His eyes were wide, and I'm certain mine were even wider. "Jefe," I shouted over the prop vibration and the roar of the airstream, "get out the mayday call."

"Mayday, mayday," Jeff called over the international emergency radio frequency of 243 MHz. "Kilo Romeo nine-one-nine. We are going down."

I switched the radar transponder from standby to 7700 and emergency. Now we would appear as a flashing symbol on any radar screen in range.

I knew from my training that I had to keep the crew working as a team, to keep their thoughts focused and their emotions in check. I immediately called out over the PA "Prepare to bailout, prepare to bailout!" Johnny would be pulling the backenders together, preparing for bailout. He was the jump master, and everything would be done just as we'd practiced so many times. My job now was to keep this crippled plane in the air long enough for them to get their parachutes on, line up, and prepare to jump. We had reviewed the procedure that morning before takeoff.

My eye again shot to the right airspeed indicator. The needle was winding counterclockwise from 150 toward 140 knots, approaching stall speed, yet the gyro and VSI showed we were still nose down, undoubtedly dropping much faster. What was going on?

"Jefe," I called, "what are you showing for airspeed?"

"I'm showing it pegged."

His instrument read 500 knots, but that was also impossible. Debris must have damaged both pitot tubes that protruded into the airstream near the missing nose cone and fed air to our airspeed indicators. I would have to fly without precise airspeed, relying on my gut feelings to keep from stalling or overspeeding the airplane.

The shaking from engine number one had not diminished. The engine instruments showed the prop blades still spinning at 30 percent rpm. I yelled to Senior, "It's failed to feather."

Senior reached over Wendy to the upper left panel and raised the clear plastic guard shield on the number one engine electric feather button. He stabbed the button, reset it, and jabbed it again. The prop would not feather electrically to minimize the drag. Senior ducked back behind us to check circuit breakers.

I had a sickening feeling that the collision had overstressed the propeller shaft hub and stripped its gears. The four big alloy blades of engine one were flat to the airstream, still connected to the turbine, which itself was no longer producing thrust after Wendy had pulled the E handle.

With the windmilling blades still turning the turbine at 30 percent rpm, and with the nose cone missing, we had maximum drag at the end of the left wing and at the front of the plane. And that drag was pulling us out of the air. We were still losing altitude at 3,500 feet a minute and were now approaching 10,000 feet, if I could trust that instrument. I had to stop this sink rate.

I needed airspeed. Again, taking the chance to lift my left hand off the chattering control yoke, I firewalled the three good engines, jamming their power levers full forward, right past military power, the ultimate in thrust.

My eye shot from the view outside the windscreen to

the vertical speed indicator, then to the gyro, then to the altimeter. For the first time, I noticed a pair of thick black cannon plugs from the now vanished weather radar, still attached to their insulated cables, wildly slapping my windscreen. That was the least of my worries.

Now I eased the control yoke toward my chest, terribly aware of the handgrips' weird vertical angle. I had to pull us out slowly and steadily. The EP-3E airframe is limited to a stress load of three and a half G's before it suffers structural damage. We'd already exceeded that load. And I had no idea what debris might have struck the elevators in the tail. I did not want to rip off a stabilizer after surviving this long.

The VSI needle crawled upward. At an altitude of about 8,000 feet, the instruments matched what I could see out the windscreen. Miraculously, we were flying straight and level. But if anything, the jolting chatter of engine number one's damaged prop was even worse. Holding the control yoke turned full right, with my leg thrust down on the right rudder pedal just to keep the nose and wings level, was horribly discouraging.

My stomach did another flip. I wondered, How long can I keep us in the sky?

chapter eighteen

Still gripping the yoke with all my strength, praying that the plane would remain level, I turned to Pat Honeck and Senior Mellos in desperation. Pat was snapping the chest buckle of his parachute harness. "Do you want to bail out or ditch this thing?" I asked.

"Will it fly?" Pat said.

"I'm not sure," I answered. "I think so."

"Let's try landing it," Pat shouted in my ear.

He was no doubt thinking the same thing I was. There was only one way to bail out of an EP-3E: through the main door at the port side aft. But no P-3C aircrew of any country in the world had ever bailed out of the aircraft. Even navy SEALs, free-fall experts, found the P-3C the roughest plane they had ever jumped. Because of the low wings, the only way the crew could exit without hitting the tail was to pull back the power on number two, the second engine in from the left, to ease the prop blast. If I attempted that with the runaway number one prop, we would roll uncontrollably again. And I didn't have enough altitude to recover.

Bailout posed another hazard. Even if most of the crew safely exited the plane at this speed and pulled their parachute ripcords, they would be strung out over miles of the South China Sea, floating in their LPUs among the sharks until rescued. Johnny could dump the big life-raft packs before he jumped, but the rafts would still fall far short of the crew members. And there were no American search-and-rescue forces in the immediate area.

Ditching was another kind of suicide. Even if the plane hadn't been so horribly ripped up, I'd learned in simulators that landing on water was extremely difficult. With the bulbous Big Look radar protruding from the belly, ditching required exacting airmanship, using our landing flaps with precision and carefully nursing the airspeed into a nose-high near-stall before letting the tail slice into the water first to slow the contact with the ocean.

I knew I couldn't do much precision flying when it took all my strength just to hold the yoke steady so the ailerons would be level. And I certainly couldn't use the engines in any delicate maneuver. We needed this amount of power just to maintain our airspeed . . . whatever that was.

Then, of course, there was the question of flaps. That

Finback had showered the bottom of the left wing with sharp debris, and I had felt his tail smack the left aileron and undercarriage before falling away. The left flap was probably damaged. If I tried dropping flaps and only one extended, the plane would again become unflyable. Changing flight characteristics in any way would probably send us out of control. However we set this airplane down—on water or land—it was going to have to be a no-flapper.

Then I visualized the gaping hole in the nose where the streamlined cone had shielded the weather radar. Above a certain speed, water was as hard as concrete. Even if we somehow managed to belly-in to the ocean without immediately flipping over, when our hacked-off snout hit the sea at 130 knots, that concave gap in front of the flight station would act as a scoop, pitching us forward with such violence that most of the crew would be killed.

I cringed at that scenario. It was best to try to find some land to put us down on. If we missed and had to ditch at sea, that would be slightly preferable to jumping from the plane—maybe.

I flipped the intercom to Navigator and called Regina. "Get us to the nearest landing strip, Reggie." I knew it had to be on the Chinese island of Hainan, probably at Lingsui, where that Finback was based.

We were either going to land on a runway in a hostile and unpredictable country, find a way to bail out, or ditch in the ocean. This was what I called a no-win situation.

"We've got cherry lights," Wendy suddenly announced, her voice thick with anxiety.

I saw the three red overheat lights on the engine gauges. We had flown too long with the engines firewalled. If we didn't ease back on the power quickly, we might blow a turbine. And this plane would definitely not be flyable if we had to shut down another engine, especially if it was engine number two on the left wing.

I flipped the switch on the inertial navigation repeater located on the center console to display my ground speed. This speed did not take into account tailwinds or headwinds at this altitude, but the instrument's digits gave me my only estimate of what my airspeed was: approximately 320 knots. We were certainly safe from a stall.

"Military power," I told Wendy.

She pulled the power levers back, and the cherry lights blinked out one by one. Normally, we could only fly at this power setting for thirty minutes without causing turbine wear. But this was not a normal day, and I cared about airspeed, not wear and tear on the turbines.

"Activate the emergency destruction plan," I called over the PA, "and prepare to ditch.

"Jefe," I said, "get me the ditching checklist." Most of the items he read did not apply to this real-world emergency. With the gaping holes in the pressure bulkhead, there was no need to depressurize, and we wouldn't be using any flaps. With two airspeed indicators that didn't work, ditching speed would have to be a guess. The only items that really applied were setting condition five at the appropriate time with the backenders' seats locked facing back and the whole crew's harnesses locked down tight. At least we were making an effort. But I knew that effort would not change what we faced.

I couldn't see what was going on at the back end, but I imagined there was some frantic activity. Operators and technicians would snatch up their binders of classified information, and Johnny would collect them in the crypto boxes he had used to carry the material aboard the aircraft that morning. Johnny would also supervise erasing any classified digital information on the built-in computers. Then he would continue the emergency destruction checklist by smashing the laptop computers with a fire axe. The final item on Johnny's checklist was dumping the boxes of classified material and smashed computers out the starboard hatch. We were well out to sea. The boxes would sink, and the paper on which the classified information was written would quickly dissolve.

It was a crazy kind of chaos on board. In back, Johnny and his group were deliberately and frantically destroying everything in sight, while in front Pat, Senior, Jeff, and I were, with equal desperation, trying to save what had already been badly damaged.

I knew that they were concerned about my prepare-to-ditch order. I hadn't changed my mind about trying to land on Hainan Island, but I had to keep all options open. In the inverted dive after the collision, we'd probably reached speeds over 400 knots and had definitely been battered by G forces well above the plane's design limits. The rugged P-3C airframe had simply not been designed for a 130-degree bank angle, so it was possible the plane had suffered major structural damage.

My mind, in fact, was filled with lots of what-ifs, none of them pretty. The constantly hammering number one prop might shake loose, causing additional damage that could send us into the ocean immediately, either in a semi-controlled ditching attempt or an out-of-control crash. Maybe a weakened hydraulic line—possibly up in the nose-wheel steering—would split and we'd lose all our hydraulic fluid and with it hydraulic boost, the airplane's equivalent of a car's power steering. Then I could never keep control with the savage drag on the left wing and the need to maintain a high airspeed to prevent stalling. If that particular malfunction hit us, I'd have to try bailing out the crew with this power setting on the engines, then ditch the plane myself. Some of the crew might make it. But I knew I didn't stand much chance.

Giving up at this point was not an option. The navy did not train its pilots to quit. I would try to hold the crew together to fly this airplane as long as that was physically possible.

As my hands gripped the yoke, my eyes scanned the

horizon for any sign of Hainan Island. Our best hope of surviving was to make an emergency landing at an airfield. The emergency destruction plan was well under way far out to sea. We were doing everything we were supposed to. The United States was not at war with China. There was nothing to be gained from our dying if we could save the airplane and the crew.

"Reggie," I called again, "give me a heading, I need a heading to land now."

"About two-nine-zero," she answered, which meant 290 degrees, close to due west.

We had come out of the dive flying almost due west, 270 degrees. All I had to do was ease the nose right 20 degrees to be on a rough course to Lingsui military airfield on Hainan. I began to pray silently. I estimated that all we had to stay in the air was another twenty minutes.

"Lingsui, Lingsui," I called on the international emergency frequency. "Mayday. Kilo Romeo nine-one-nine. We are a severely damaged aircraft. We are about seventy nautical miles southeast of Hainan. Request permission to make emergency landing."

Through the engine roar and screaming airstream whipping around my legs and chest, I heard no reply. I frantically repeated the call, making sure I was transmitting on the correct radio and frequency.

Again I heard no reply, not even a crackle of static. Were they not getting the message, or were they just stonewalling me? I knew we would have to land whether they answered or not. It was as simple—and as complicated—as that.

My arms and shoulders were cramping with the strain of holding the chattering yoke at this angle. "Jefe, I need to get in the other seat."

I nodded to Pat and down to the controls, indicating I wanted him to swap out for me while I pulled on my chute and traded places with Jeff in the left seat.

Senior Mellos emerged from the alternative circuit breaker panel behind my seat. He was not wearing his parachute. Probably thinks he's going to ride this thing down with me, I thought.

"Senior," I ordered, "get your chute on."

"Roger that, sir."

chapter nineteen

"You've got the controls, Jefe," I yelled, watching to make sure he could hold the yoke and rudder hard right. Then I popped my harness and jumped out of the right seat. Pat Honeck was back in that seat with the harness locked moments later.

"Oh, my God," Pat moaned in disbelief as he took the controls from Jeff Vignery and felt the strain for the first time.

"You got it, Pat?" I couldn't let the plane roll again.

"Yeah," he answered with grim determination.

Johnny Comerford suddenly appeared in the narrow aisle behind the flight station. He wore his helmet, parachute, and Nomex fire-resistant gloves. His face was bathed in sweat.

He helped me into my parachute, but my hands were shaking too badly to snap the lower buckles. "Joh . . ." I tried to speak, but my tongue suddenly stuck to my palate. My mouth was parched from the explosive decompression and the adrenaline still surging through me. I grabbed my water bottle and chugged down half. "Johnny, help me here."

He bent to snap the harness buckles. I didn't want to wear the chute because I knew there was no way I could leave the flight station after the rest of the crew had jumped and successfully work my way aft to jump myself. The autopilot could never hold the plane, and the moment I released the controls, the plane would snap-roll left again, all the way into a full inverted spin, and I'd be plastered to the deck like a squashed bug on the windshield of a Nebraska farm truck. But I had just ordered Senior to put on his chute, so it would be bad for morale if I didn't do the same. This was not a suicide mission. We were still U.S. Navy aviators, and I was determined to save as many of my crew as I could.

"I'm ready to pop the hatch," Johnny shouted over the surrounding roar. Neither of us was wearing a headset.

I nodded vigorously and yelled back, "Do what you have to do. I don't care when you pop it. We're heading to Lingsui."

I finished my water and swapped with Jeff to fly from the left seat. Senior Mellos had already swapped out with

Wendy in the flight engineer's seat. Out the left window, I now could clearly see the damage to the number one prop tips, even though the blades were still windmilling at 30 percent rpm. In the blurred disk, it looked like about a foot had been chewed off two of them. No wonder the plane was shaking itself apart. We had to get on the ground before that prop threw a blade like a 150-pound sword through our fuselage.

I took another breath. We were probably only 40 miles from land now. Another ten to twelve minutes to go, I thought, unless the Chinese deliberately try to keep us from landing. Even without official permission, I was determined to put my wheels on their airfield. It was the only chance we had.

I pulled on the headset, took over the jolting yoke from Pat, and looked to my right. Would Senior and Pat obey an order to bail out while I stayed behind to fly the plane alone? I hoped I wouldn't have to face that question.

Pat was repeatedly calling Lingsui directly on the emergency frequency. There was still no answer. I felt the cabin pressure change, and I knew Johnny had pulled open the starboard overwing hatch to dump out classified material. A few minutes later, I felt the hatch snap shut. I assumed he had discarded everything he was supposed to.

Our altimeter, the instrument that told us our altitude, had suddenly stopped functioning, with the needle wobbling well above and then below 8,000 feet, even though the horizon and our other instruments told us we were flying level and not sinking. I wasn't too worried because we still had our radar altimeter, which would begin giving a precise readout once we reached 5,000 feet.

I knew from studying maps that Hainan had a tall central mountain that should be visible at this altitude and distance, but there was just too much haze to provide the visibility we needed. I wanted to slow down and gradually bleed off some altitude as we approached the island because I wasn't sure of our final heading to Lingsui.

"Reggie," I called, "where's this field?"

"Hold two-nine-zero until we can see the island," she answered.

I decided to start our descent now. The engines were still near maximum power. I took the three power levers in my right hand while I gripped the badly vibrating yoke in my left. The levers responded with another 1,000 shaft horsepower. Suddenly the horizon tilted viciously and the left wing and nose dropped sharply. Shocked by the abrupt altitude loss, I shoved the power levers forward again and felt the airspeed overcome drag as the props took hold. The descent would have to be a lot more gradual if we were going to keep this plane under control.

"Set condition five," I told Pat. "We're going to try to land."

Pat punched the PA button to relay the order. "Set condition five."

That meant everybody was in their seat with their harnesses buckled tight. I pulled back on the power levers in tiny increments until we could hold a slow rate of descent. My arms were exhausted, so Pat and I took turns at the controls, each managing to hold the wings level and keep us on our heading for three or four minutes at a time.

As we reached the denser, more humid air around 5,000 feet, we found we could carefully turn the yoke left from the vertical position back to about 75 degrees, making it somewhat easier to fly the airplane. But with the continuous jackhammer vibration, the work was still incredibly tiring.

Finally, the pale green hump of Hainan Island emerged through the solid haze ahead. I was overjoyed. I had the controls, and Pat made the radio calls.

"Lingsui," he said twice, speaking clearly and slowly. "Kilo Romeo nine-one-nine declaring an emergency. We are a severely damaged aircraft approximately five miles south of Hainan. We need to land immediately."

There was still no reply.

As we neared the coast, the white jumble of a small city shimmered through the haze directly ahead of us. Navy pilots do not fly crippled airplanes over cities. I added a little power and turned into a shallow right bank, away from the island. It made me angry we weren't getting any help from the control tower. They had to have heard us, I thought; they could give us a heading. Instead, they were

149

playing with our lives. We would have to fly a circle out here until we had a better idea of where the Lingsui airfield was.

On our mission we always flew with approach plates for the major airports in the area, but no one had anticipated we'd be trying to set down our crippled airplane at a Chinese military airfield. We had no idea of the exact heading, runway lengths, or any ground obstacles we had to clear before landing.

As we flew this slow circle, descending to about 2,000 feet above the sea, Regina would use her precision navigation equipment to give us an approach.

"Reggie," I asked her, "will you punch me direct?"

"You should see a city," she said cautiously, "then a river. The field is just to the left there."

Completing the 360-degree turn, I leaned forward and saw two green hills to the west and a curving beach northeast of the city. The scene looked like Kaneohe Bay on Oahu. The tan line of a concrete runway stood out beyond the first green hill.

"Lingsui," I called again. "I have the field in sight."

As we crossed the white crescent of the beach at 1,000 feet, I tried to turn the wheel of the elevator trim tab. It wouldn't budge. Another flood of adrenaline washed over me. As I'd feared, something was damaged on the tail. Don't force it, I thought, so I gave up trying to turn the elevator.

Senior Mellos had been watching intently as Pat and I flew, scanning every instrument to make sure the good engines were performing as well as they could. All three of us on the flight station were absorbed with the landing we would soon have to attempt.

"I don't think we want to move these flaps," I said, looking out at my wings.

"Roger that," they replied almost in unison.

"Senior," I asked, "what are my speeds?"

As we approached the island, he had been methodically paging through the NATOPS, searching for solutions to our landing problems. Apparently the scenario that combined an unfeathered, windmilling prop, nonfunctioning airspeed indicators, a missing nose cone, and a no-flap landing was not in the book. None of us wanted to think about any damage that the nose wheel or its strut might also have suffered when the Finback's forward fuselage slammed into our nose.

Crossing the palm groves and tan squares of the dry rice paddies at 1,000 feet, the ground speed registered 220 knots. We could probably trust that as a reasonable guess.

"A hundred and forty-three knots is our no-flap landing speed," Senior said.

Since I had no way to judge our exact airspeed, we'd have to fly the final approach faster. "We'll add thirty knots to that," I said.

I hoped we would not really be setting this damaged plane down at an airspeed of 173 knots, but I had the queasy feeling that we'd be going just that fast.

We still had almost 15 tons of jet fuel aboard. If the nose wheel collapsed on landing, the crash and explosion would be more catastrophic than swerving off a runway with blown tires on takeoff.

My course was set, though. I was going to try to land on a solid runway. For the moment I needed more speed to get us to there, so I bumped the power levers forward an inch, and our ground speed increased.

The shimmering runway stretched out ahead, perpendicular to our flight path. I wanted to cross the airfield at this angle, flying at about 800 feet, so I could inspect the field. But after I crossed the runway, I would have to bank 30 degrees left into the dead engine to avoid the steep green slope of a hill. Back at Whidbey Island, flying an undamaged airplane with four good engines, I wouldn't have thought twice about the maneuver. That day, struggling with the thrashing control yoke to reach but not exceed the proper angle of bank left me sweating.

We crossed the airfield at an altitude of about 700 feet. There were no airplanes or vehicles on the runway. To the right I caught a glimpse of open aircraft revetments, or barricades, each enclosing an F-8 II Finback.

I held my breath as I banked left to avoid the green slope.

"Gear down," I told Pat, and added automatically, "Landing checklist."

Pat's hands stabbed down on either side of his seat. "Where's the checklist?" he asked frantically.

The checklist had been snatched up and dumped with the classified material in the flight station.

"Pat," I said, "we've got condition five set in the back end. Flaps are going to stay up. Get the gear down!"

Pat reached down to grab the tire-shaped knob of the gear handle and pulled it down. All three of us watched as the landing gear position indicator on the right panel clicked from up to down. The familiar rumble was much louder with the nose cone missing. The landing gear did not seem to have been damaged.

For the first time since the collision, the tight coil of fear inside my chest relaxed—just a little. We're going to live, I thought.

"And now we've got three down and locked," I called out, meaning all the wheels were in place.

"Yeah, right," Pat said, the relief clear in his voice even through the roar of the airstream, "okay."

I rolled out of the turn at about 500 feet and headed toward north to turn again onto final approach. I had no idea what the winds were, since we hadn't been able to speak to the tower. There had been no marker boards indicating the runway's distance, but it looked long enough to handle us, since it was an F-8 base. It would have to be, because we were landing.

Gripping the shuddering yoke only as tightly as I had to, I rolled back the plane to line up with the runway.

"Keep calling out my ground speed to me until we're on the runway," I said to Pat.

I wanted to keep the nose pitched down for a clear view of the runway. Once I came over the runway, I'd level off and chop the power to let the plane settle. Because of the damage to the fuselage, I didn't want to fly a standard, nose-high approach, touching the rear wheels down first for aerodynamic braking before dropping the nose gear onto the pavement. That would make for a much longer landing, and the chance for more things to go wrong. I wanted to stop the plane as soon as I could. Much as a Tomcat pilot hit the deck of a carrier, I would try to stick the landing. At least I didn't have to try to snag an arresting wire. I had some flexibility, but I knew there would be no chance to fly a touch-and-go. The drag from the number one prop and the severed nose, combined with our weight, made that impossible. I had to get this airplane down safely on the runway the first time around.

"One seventy-five," Pat intoned, "one seventy . . . one sixty-five." The runway rushed toward us. I kept both hands on the chattering yoke but was ready to chop power with my right hand.

"One-seventy," Pat announced. "Whoa."

The wide concrete blocks of the runway were suddenly beneath us. I eased back on the yoke and pulled the three power levers back to flight idle. The big airplane settled so gently, we could hardly feel the wheels touch. I was amazed our touchdown could be so smooth after all the turbulence in the air.

We were still moving at about 170 knots. I looked ahead of me. The runway wasn't that long. I estimated that we had about fifteen seconds to slow the heavy aircraft. I waited for the green beta lights to blink on to show that the prop pitch of the spooled-down engines had safely reached less than 10 degrees; if they were more than 10 degrees, the plane would tend to swerve. Then I gripped the three good power levers and pulled them into reverse, pumping the rudder to keep us on a reasonably straight path. The plane felt squirrelly, but we were slowing fast.

"I've got it," I said, as much to reassure myself as the others. "I've got it."

When I felt the rudder going dead, I continued holding the centerline by fanning the power levers and then took over control with nose-wheel steering. I was conscious of the stunned silence in the flight station, even though 50 knots of wind was still blasting through the ripped pressure bulkhead.

Suddenly, as the plane rolled to a stop, the silence ended. I could hear the crew in the back end screaming and cheering with joy. I released a deep sigh as I thought, I cannot believe we're alive. I turned to silently share the miracle with Senior and Pat. They both gave me stunned, disbelieving smiles. Our ordeal had lasted about thirty-three minutes. It was the longest half hour I had ever spent in my life. I just can't believe we're alive, I thought again.

Then another, colder thought struck me. We're alive, but we're also in Communist China.

chapter twenty

As we neared the end of the runway, a small man stood on the tarmac and angrily waved us onto a ramp. I followed his directions and came to a stop, but I kept the engines running. Suddenly, on my left, I saw two open green military trucks full of uniformed soldiers, many with AK-47 assault rifles.

As the soldiers jumped out and began to circle the plane, I got on the intercom. "Ballgame," I asked Johnny Comerford in the back end, "have you been able to call our chain of command to report that we're safe on the deck?"

"Not yet," he replied immediately. "Give me a minute, okay?"

On the other side of the runway, I noticed some mildewed concrete buildings with orange tile roofs and stands of palms. On the surrounding hills were dry rice paddies and thatched houses. A few civilians could be seen working in the fields.

When I looked back toward the soldiers, our taxi man was pointing at each engine and slicing his hand across his throat, telling me to cut the power.

"Senior," I said, "shut down number four."

As the propeller on engine four came slowly to a halt, I was determined to keep the other two engines running in order to buy Johnny more time. It was essential that our command receive word directly from us about the midair collision before we exited the plane.

A minute later Johnny told me he had made contact with the U.S. military, and Senior shut down the last two engines. In the distance I watched as a military twin-prop aircraft took off over the ocean, probably to look for the downed pilot. Even though his reckless flying had almost killed us, I hoped he would be found alive.

I moved toward the rear of the plane for one last check. The deck was littered with smashed glass and torn wiring from the surveillance equipment that had been destroyed. When I looked at the faces of my crew, I mostly saw relief mixed with fear.

I pulled off my parachute and survival vest and tried to compose myself before I met my host. I was the mission commander; it was my job to protect my crew and our aircraft. When I opened the door, I found Chinese soldiers clustered below, including an officer and his interpreter. In halting English the interpreter asked if we needed medical assistance. When I told him no, he asked if anyone was carrying a weapon. I answered him truthfully again. We had no weapons.

Then the officer ordered everyone off the plane.

I argued that my crew and I weren't leaving until I first spoke to my commanding officer in Kadena. My response irritated the officer, and I could feel the tension rise in the hot, muggy air. Every time my eyes swept over the rifle-carrying soldiers, I reminded myself to be careful. We had completed the emergency destruction plan and had no choice but to exit the plane.

One by one, the crew climbed down the ladder that extended from the aircraft. Some were clearly intimidated by the armed soldiers. Others kept their faces calm and neutral.

"Everything did go all right in the back end, right?" I whispered to Johnny, to reassure myself that any confidential material had been destroyed and the United States knew about our location.

"Everything's good back there."

"Okay," I said as Pat joined our discussion. We were out of earshot of the Chinese. "We're still on the mission," I said. "Just so we don't confuse the crew and also the Chinese, I'm still the mission commander. That could change if things get physical and they start treating us like POWs."

They both agreed. Under the military code of conduct, the senior ranking officer assumed command of all prisoners of war held at a particular site. And Pat Honeck, while also a lieutenant, had more time in service than I did, which made him senior to me. But I didn't consider ourselves to be POWs yet. The collision with the Finback had been an accident caused by poor airmanship and aggressive flying, not an act of war. At this stage, I could not imagine that the Chinese would find a reason to keep us there very long. I would soon find out how wrong I was.

A medium-sized bus had pulled up beside us. Before boarding it, I told my crew they'd all done an exceptional job in an extraordinary crisis, and I was proud of every one of them. I added that we would now need to keep the faith, but if we stuck together, we would get through the ordeal ahead of us. Some of the crew looked just tired, while others were visibly anxious. I hoped I sounded reassuring.

The bus took us to an old concrete-block building, the airfield's mess hall, where we ate boiled rice and chunks of tasteless fish while guards paced back and forth behind us. After the meal, we were escorted to another concrete two-story building and told to pick rooms on the second floor. The hall bathrooms were filthy and everyone's bedding unwashed, but at least all of us would be on one floor. I chose Johnny and Pat as my roommates so we could discuss strategy. I assumed the rooms were bugged, and cautioned everyone to be discreet.

I confided some of my worries to Pat and Johnny. Nobody had any idea how long we would be in China or what the repercussions would be for us. After the three of us met with Senior and one of our petty officers, we decided to set up a watch. Two people would stay awake to serve as watchdogs while the rest of us got some badly needed sleep. After an hour, the two would be relieved by another pair, and so on, until we got through the night.

Later that evening, I tried in vain to sleep. Nightmare images of the collision kept popping into my head. Reliving the traumatic thirty-three minutes, I knew there was nothing I could or would have done differently. Around midnight, our Chinese liaison officer, who asked us to call him Lieutenant Tony, burst into my room and shook my shoulder.

"Lieutenant Osborn," he said excitedly, "we must talk to you."

I followed Lieutenant Tony down the hall and into a large, brightly lit room with video cameras and lights on tripods. Two interpreters sat beside two senior officers behind a table. I dropped into an uncomfortable chair facing the table and the video cameras.

Squinting into the floodlights, I realized I had been awake for almost twenty-four hours. And from the way this room had been set up, I knew this interrogation would not be brief. They had chosen the middle of the night, expecting I'd be at my weakest.

Through an interpreter, the first officer identified himself as the base commander. "We are here to investigate your ramming of our aircraft," he began in a harsh voice. "We lost the pilot and have yet to find him. We need to find details of your mission for investigation. Are you willing to give us names and positions of every person on board?"

I answered that I would provide the names of our crew, but first I wanted to talk to the American ambassador in Beijing.

The base commander angrily dismissed my request and began to hammer me with more questions and accusations. "Why did you ram our plane? We have witnesses."

I knew then that either the pilot of the surviving Finback had been too embarrassed to tell his superiors what had really happened to cause the collision, or if he had told them, the Chinese officials had refused to accept his account. After all, this was a terrible embarrassment for the Chinese. The United States had been protesting the erratic and dangerous flying of Chinese pilots near our aircraft for months, but the Lingsui pilots had ignored it. Now one of them was missing, an American aircrew had narrowly escaped with their lives, and a crippled EP-3E sat on the Lingsui taxi ramp like a beached whale. It was clear that to protect their international reputation, the Chinese were going to try to shift the blame and force me or my crew into admitting we had caused the accident.

I would not cave in and give them what they wanted.

I stayed calm, spoke in clear, short sentences, and gave them a detailed account of the collision.

"Liar!" the base commander bellowed, slapping the table. "You had better tell the truth . . . for the safety of your family, and your crew, and yourself. You must cooperate with this investigation, Lieutenant Osborn. Why did you engage in espionage against the Chinese people? You are a master spy."

Through the glare of harsh lights, I again gave my version, the truthful version. I refused to be intimidated. Again, they tried to bully me into admitting I had either strayed into Chinese airspace or deliberately rammed their pilot.

This session lasted over five and a half hours. Later I would learn that other interrogators had taken Senior and Pat to separate rooms to barrage them with similar questions and threats. None of us had given an inch; we'd stuck to the truth.

The Chinese officers wanted to interrogate me again the next morning, but Pat and Johnny insisted I was too exhausted. While I was left alone to sleep, Jeff and Regina were questioned in front of the ever-present video cameras. The Chinese were probing for our weakest link. If they found the chink in the armor, they would come back and pound the rest of us until they got a group confession.

At five-thirty that afternoon, I was taken to a different room. Once again the base commander showered me with questions. They wanted to break me in the worst way, I thought. As the pressure intensified, I remembered not only my training in the frozen Maine woods, but the cool, strong presence of one of my mentors, Lieutenant Norm Maxim.

Norm, I knew, would have stayed one step ahead of his captors, assessing their strengths and weaknesses. And it was clear to me that the Chinese position was full of holes. I had explained that I was on autopilot while the Finbacks harassed us, so it would have been impossible to swing my plane into one of their fuselages. I had other persuasive arguments too, and I knew if I stuck to them, stuck to the facts, the Chinese would have to find another tactic.

But not that day. The furious base commander was determined to wear me down. He looked at me harshly. "Lieutenant Osborn, you will not be allowed to see your crew or anyone else until you cooperate. You need time alone to think."

The guards took me a small room that was air-conditioned, the temperature seemingly set at subzero. Outside it was dark, and I had no idea of the time.

I would not know until later that my disappearance caused Jeff, Pat, Johnny, and Senior deep concern. When it came time for dinner, speaking for the entire crew, they told the guards that no one would go to the mess hall to eat unless I joined them. We knew our captors wanted all of us to appear healthy; otherwise the outside world would see we'd been treated badly. That knowledge was a bargaining chip for us. As the situation required, Pat had now assumed his role as senior ranking officer. He threatened the Chinese with an outright hunger strike by the entire crew.

After more arguing, the base commander allowed Pat and Johnny to visit me in my freezing room. They woke me gently and told me about the hunger strike. I agreed with the idea. It was the only leverage we had.

After they left, the night seemed endless. Whenever I fell asleep, the guards would scrape their chairs and blow smoke in my face. They were trying to break my will through sleep deprivation and harassment. Well, I thought, recalling those endless months in high school after the car accident when I had plucked at the inward-growing eyelashes and wondered if I would ever become a navy pilot, they didn't know how stubborn I could be.

Around eight o'clock in the morning, Lieutenant Tony arrived. "You can go to breakfast now," he informed me.

"Where's the crew?" I asked. "I'm not going anywhere without them."

Lieutenant Tony left in frustration but returned half an hour later to accompany me to the mess hall. I was happy to find the rest of the crew there. Lieutenant Tony ordered me to sit at a separate table and be silent, but I just ignored him and sat next to Johnny and asked about the crew.

Back at the barracks, a rear admiral demanded more details of the collision. Over and over, I told him I had nothing new to add. When he saw I was adamant, he threatened the safety of my crew and me again.

After several hours, with my head throbbing, the base commander shifted tactics. He asked if I'd like to see my plane.

"Sure," I said, eager for a break. Then he said he wanted to inspect the plane with me. It was obvious this would be another chance for them to distort the truth. I told him he could not board the plane because it was U.S. government property. Then I offered a compromise: "I'll go with you to the airplane only if I can see an American representative." He quickly agreed.

Once Regina, Senior, and I were driven to the plane, we were greeted by a host of Chinese reporters and cameramen. The admiral faced the cameras and wasted no time accusing my crew of violating Chinese airspace and ramming his plane, killing the pilot. I was frustrated by his lies and again insisted that no one enter the plane. I didn't want to be portrayed on film as the "master spy" the Chinese were making me out to be. After more arguments, I finally allowed Senior to lead the admiral and his video crews on board. He could honestly answer that he knew nothing about the surveillance equipment in the back end, since it was not his main area of expertise.

While they were inside, I worked my way along the plane and surveyed the incredible damage, from the missing nose to the hacked-away metal of the propellers to the popped rivets in the tail. I thought again how lucky we'd been to land the plane. It was a living definition of a miracle. By all rights we should have been dead.

And that's when I knew: We had survived our catastrophe in the air, and so we would survive here at Lingsui.

chapter twenty-one

Later that afternoon, we were moved to a "military guest house" in Haikou, the principal city of Hainan Island. My room was a small suite, a big improvement over the barracks at Lingsui. Lieutenant Tony's room was next door. With guards occupying the corridor, the rest of the crew was assigned to rooms down the hall.

A few hours later I met my crew in a private hotel dining room, and while nervous guards padded up and down around us, we said our customary prayers and sat down to eat. No one was allowed to talk, and my request for a meeting with my crew after dinner was firmly turned down. I was drained, having gotten a total of about four hours of real sleep since takeoff at Kadena three days before. My nerves were also on edge about the promised meeting with a representative from the American embassy. Was it really going to happen?

Around midnight, Lieutenant Tony knocked on my door. "Get up, quickly," he said. "The American representative has arrived."

Although a Chinese official would be in the room to monitor everything that was said, my spirits immediately picked up, and the crew buzzed with excitement. An hour later, under the glare of more video lamps, Brigadier General Neil Sealock, the U.S. defense attaché at our Beijing embassy, walked into the room. He was tall and square-shouldered, and his green uniform bore multiple rows of decorations and ribbons. Just seeing him filled me with hope.

"Attention on deck!" I ordered the crew.

We all rose in unison and snapped to attention.

"At ease," General Sealock said, his eyes carefully scanning the room.

Under the scrutiny of a heavyset Chinese official, General Sealock informed us the Chinese had given him only forty minutes to talk to us. The United States government, indeed the whole world, he said, knew of our situation. To know that we were on CNN every hour, as the general implied, gave me comfort. General Sealock asked us to confirm our identities by name and by place and date of birth. He told us that our families had been briefed on what had happened, that the entire country, including President

George W. Bush, was behind us, and that negotiations for our release were going on around the clock at the highest possible level.

Then he pulled out a notebook and asked each of us what we wanted to tell our loved ones back home. I was the last to go, and I gave a positive, upbeat message for my entire family.

I hoped that the end of our ordeal was near, but any optimism I had about going home proved to be premature. Our battle of wills with the Chinese only increased after the general's visit. There would be more manipulation, more interrogations, more sleepless days and nights, more efforts to separate me from my crew. I constantly had to fight the Chinese to keep any interrogations of my crew short and to the point. We were even threatened with being put on trial as international spies. The Chinese were pulling out all the stops to win a confession and apology from us. All of us were bone weary and mentally pushed to the wall, but we wouldn't give in.

I knew that the high-level negotiations between Washington and Beijing for our release centered on which country was going to apologize to the other. If my crew and I buckled under, it was obvious which side was going to win. An apology would mean that we had caused the incident, not the Chinese pilot, whose name I learned was Wang Wei. He had been a father, a husband, and a son. It was horrible that he was lost at sea. But if we were forced to apologize for the collision, we would be conceding that the false Chinese version of the incident was true. This was not acceptable.

We went on a brief hunger strike and finally won some concessions—mainly the right to get together and talk, and find ways to keep our spirits up. General Sealock came for another visit, bringing us candy and e-mails from our families—a major morale booster—and told us to keep the faith.

I found some satisfaction in writing "letters" to my loved ones, printing as well as my groggy mind allowed in the small pages of my notebook. In my letter to my mom, I said I knew how hard this situation was on her and the rest of the family. "I did what I had to do to save twenty-four lives. The fact that I am writing this letter to you today is a miracle from God Himself. Please know that I am strong, clear-minded, and will bring twenty-four men and women back to their families where they belong."

Finally, on Wednesday, April 11, the eleventh day of our detention, we were herded back into the dining room to face the admiral. I expected more harassment, but instead, reading from a prepared statement, he told us we were going to be released.

I was numb with joy. Everyone in the crew was deliriously happy. The Chinese made it seem as though they were releasing us for humanitarian reasons, but I knew otherwise. We had held out against their demands.

As we boarded a bus to leave Hainan, I realized we'd been detained for almost twelve days, during which I had accumulated a total of fifteen hours of uninterrupted sleep. During those twelve days I had tried to be an effective leader, relying on my training to be direct and straightforward with everyone. I had learned from my family to be a good judge of character, to be respectful and honest, and to hold to my convictions. I think that's what got me by. I was proud that I had endured, but I was more proud that I had protected my crew from harsh, prolonged interrogations. No one had broken and offered an apology. We were returning with our honor intact.

I later learned that the tense negotiations between the United States and China had finally ended when the Bush administration delivered a letter expressing America's sorrow at the loss of Wang Wei's life, while refusing to accept blame for the collision. The Chinese government was forced to make do with this, even though it was less than the full apology they had wanted originally. The Bush administration had held firm. Now we could go home.

We were soon flown to Hickam Air Force Base in Hawaii, where I was honored to receive a call directly from President Bush during two exhausting days of debriefing. "Shane," he said, "speaking as an old F-102 pilot, I think you did a heck of a job bringing that plane down. You made our country proud."

Before leaving, we held a brief news conference beside the navy C-9 jet transport that would carry us home to Whidbey Island. "I want to thank America, the administration, and everyone involved in getting us home so quickly," I told the reporters, and then I turned away from the microphones to face the crew members lined up behind me. "We can all be proud of this crew."

Then Senior Mellos commented on the teamwork that had saved our plane from almost certain disaster. "Thank God for the training we practice every day," he said. "Because without it, we'd have a different kind of press conference today."

A reporter asked me about the persistent Chinese demands that our government apologize for the collision. No apology was necessary, I said, because we had not been at fault. "I'm here to tell you that we did it right."

I was thrilled to be back in the United States, to have proudly served my country; and on April 14, when I flew on to Whidbey Island, the home of the VQ-1, to embrace my friends and family, I knew that the ordeal was finally over.

On May 18, my crew and I were invited to Washington for a formal visit to the White House and to meet President Bush. Afterward, we marched up to the grandstand at nearby Andrews Air Force Base. Here the crew would receive medals for our performance in the air and on Hainan Island. I would be honored with the Distinguished Flying Cross, the armed services' highest decoration for airmanship. Senior Mellos and I would also receive the Meritorious Service Medal for the leadership we had shown during the detention on Hainan. Senior and all the other members of the crew would also receive the Air Medal, recognition that they had performed skillfully and bravely in an extremely hazardous operational mission.

We lined up in our straight formation, waiting for the citations to be read and for the Chairman of the Joint Chiefs of Staff, General Henry H. Shelton, accompanied by Secretary of Defense Donald H. Rumsfeld, to present the decorations.

I had always been awed by the Distinguished Flying Cross. I wished there were some way I could share it with the rest of my crew. Instead, I would accept it in their names and in the spirit of their courageous service.

"The president of the United States takes pleasure in presenting the Distinguished Flying Cross to Lieutenant Shane J. Osborn, United States Navy. . . ." The amplified voice of the master of ceremonies carried across the concrete parking ramp toward the EP-3E that we had flown from Whidbey Island the day before. "For extraordinary achievement while participating in aerial flight . . . during sensitive surveillance operations on April 1, 2001 . . . following an in-flight collision with a People's Republic of China fighter aircraft, Lieutenant Osborn displayed superb airmanship and courage. Despite extreme damage to the aircraft . . . he heroically regained control, directed appropriate emergency procedures, and coordinated the crew's efforts to safely land the aircraft. Lieutenant Osborn's dedicated efforts ensured the survival of twenty-four crew members. . . . By his superb airmanship, proven ability to perform under pressure, and steadfast devotion to duty, Lieutenant Osborn reflected great credit upon himself and upheld the highest traditions of the United States Naval Service."

I came to attention and saluted as General Shelton pinned the two decorations to my uniform. This was a very proud moment. I suddenly remembered those sunny afternoons in Lyle Brewer's little Piper Cub over the Dakota cornfields. I recalled the hours of studying basic aeronautics in Civil Air Patrol in Norfolk. The drudgery of aviation preflight indoctrination came back, as did the tension of Lieutenant Jeff Nelson's stern flight instruction in primary and the joy of my first solo flight. The hours and hours of emergency procedure training in TC-12s flashed in vivid sequence through my mind. Then there were the days and weeks in the cockpit of the EP-3E, during which my most demanding mentor, Lieutenant Norm Maxim, had shaped me into a mature airman and a leader in his own model.

General Shelton pinned on the second decoration, and we exchanged crisp salutes. Still at attention, I glanced gratefully down the line of my crew, starting with Senior Chief Nicholas Mellos. Without them, I knew, I wouldn't have been standing there that day.

I was proud beyond words of them all—and eager to fly again soon.

afterword

For over a month after our safe return from Haikou, the Chinese and American governments negotiated the fate of our crippled EP-3E, stranded at the Lingsui air base. The Americans wanted to repair the plane and fly it out of China. The Chinese would not accept this proposal.

Finally, in late May, the two sides reached a compromise. The United States would dispatch a team of civilian technicians from the Lockheed Martin Corporation, who would disassemble the aircraft so that it could be flown out of Hainan in pieces aboard two giant Antonov 124 cargo planes leased from a Russian firm.

In mid-June, the Lockheed Martin team arrived at Lingsui to begin work. They drained the aircraft's fuel tanks, oil, and hydraulic fluid, and then packed up small equipment in crates. Next they removed the big antenna cover as well as smaller covers and antennas. The crew then removed the engines, propellers, and the tall tail assembly. Finally, the wings came off, the long lines of rivets sheared with power tools.

On July 4, 2001, the big Antonovs began shuttling their loads between Lingsui and Kadena Air Base, Okinawa, where our flight had begun. A week later, the Antonovs landed at Dobbins Air Force Base, near the Lockheed Martin factory in Marietta, Georgia.

The EP-3E is still being analyzed to determine whether it can be safely rebuilt to fly again.

Meanwhile, the Chinese submitted a bill for $1 million to the U.S. government to cover expenses associated with our detention on Hainan and the recovery of our aircraft. The American embassy in Beijing called the bill "highly exaggerated." And the U.S. House of Representatives voted 424 to 6 against giving the Chinese any compensation at all for expenses related to our detention or the return of the EP-3E surveillance plane.

The issue remains unresolved.

glossary of aviation terms

AEROBATIC FLIGHT - Maneuvers in which an aircraft departs from normal flight attitudes to perform rolls, loops, and dives while remaining under control.

AILERON - One of an aircraft's moveable control surfaces, located on the outer trailing edge of each wing, which controls the angle of bank or roll.

AIRFRAME - The basic structure of an aircraft: the fuselage, wings, tail, etc., excluding the engines, instruments, and nonstructural internal equipment.

AIRSPEED - The speed of an aircraft through the surrounding air, which, because of the effect of winds, does not necessarily reflect the aircraft's speed across the ground below (ground speed).

ANGLE OF ATTACK (AOA) - The angular distance of an aircraft's lifting surfaces (wings, etc.) above the horizontal. Too high an angle of attack at too low an airspeed will result in a stall.

ATTITUDE - The position of an aircraft in flight relative to the earth, i.e., wings level, nose high, nose down, inverted, etc.

BANK - A maneuver controlled by the ailerons in which an aircraft dips one wing while raising the other; the basic method of changing horizontal direction. In straight and level flight, an aircraft has a 0-degree angle of bank; fully inverted, the bank angle is 180 degrees. Aircraft are limited by design from exceeding certain angles of bank.

COCKPIT (flight station or flight deck) - The position at the front of

179

an aircraft from which the pilot(s) operate the controls. On older, multiengine aircraft, a flight engineer may also work in the cockpit.

CONTROL SURFACES - Moveable sections on the wings and tail—ailerons, elevators, and rudder—that permit an aircraft to maneuver.

DRAG - The force holding back an aircraft in flight from forward or vertical movement. Modern aircraft are designed to minimize drag.

ELEVATORS - Moveable control surfaces on the trailing edge of an aircraft's horizontal tail that govern the angle of attack.

FEATHER (propellers) - To manipulate the blades of a propeller of a shut-down engine so that they are edge-on to the airstream in order to minimize drag.

FIREWALL - Aviator's jargon for the emergency use of maximum engine power exceeding military power.

FLAPS - A pair of matched extendable panels on the wings' trailing edges. At takeoff and landing, and at slower speeds, flaps increase the wings' surface and thus increase lift, but also increase drag. Flaps are used to slow the aircraft for landing.

FUSELAGE - The tubular or cylindrical body of an aircraft to which the wings and tail are attached.

G FORCES (G's) - The forces an aircraft and its occupants experience during flight maneuvers. One G equals the normal force of gravity. G's can be either positive or negative.

GROUND SPEED - An aircraft's true speed across the ground, which, because of the effect of winds, may differ from airspeed.

HF - High-frequency radio, used for long-distance communication.

HYDRAULIC SYSTEM - An aircraft's "power steering," which uses hydraulic fluid under pressure to move control surfaces.

LEADING EDGE - The forward edge of the wing or the tail's horizontal stabilizer.

LIFT - The lifting force generated by an aircraft's aerodynamic surfaces, especially in the wings and tail.

MAYDAY - An international emergency distress radio call, which an aircraft usually makes over the Guard Channel frequency of 121.5 or 243 MHz.

MILITARY POWER - The maximum nonemergency power setting for the engines of military propeller-driven aircraft.

MUSHY - Flight aviator's jargon for unstable flight, usually resulting from flying too slowly at too high an angle of attack.

NOSE CONE - A streamlined cone at the front of an aircraft, usually covering a radar antenna.

PITCH - The angle of an aircraft's nose relative to the horizon, which is controlled by the elevators.

PITOT TUBE - A hollow tube mounted on an aircraft's fuselage that feeds air to an instrument, especially the airspeed indicator.

POWER LEVEL - Also called the throttle on many aircraft: the engine control that governs the amount of fuel an engine receives (especially turbine engines).

PROPELLER PITCH - The angle or "bite" of propeller blades relative to the airstream.

RADOME (radar dome) - A streamlined covering or fairing for a radar antenna.

ROLL - An aircraft's tilting movement (bank) during which one wing dips and the other rises; rolls can accompany dives and climbs, especially during aerobatic or uncontrolled flight.

RUDDER - The large control surface in the tail's vertical stabilizer, which governs an aircraft's sideways movement. The pilot controls the rudder by pushing the right or left rudder pedal.

SNAP ROLL - A sudden, extreme roll maneuver. A snap roll will usually exceed the safe angle of bank of all aircraft except those designed for aerobatic flight.

STABILIZER - One of the T-shaped surfaces of an aircraft's tail; there are usually two horizontal and one vertical stabilizers.

STALL - Loss of lift with resulting loss of control that occurs when an aircraft flies either at too high an angle of attack or too slowly, or a combination of both.

STICK - Sometimes called the control stick: a device used principally in smaller aircraft to control roll and pitch. Moving the stick sideways activates the ailerons; pushing and pulling the stick activates the elevators.

TRAILING EDGE - The aft (rear) edge of a wing or horizontal stabilizer.

TURBOPROP - An aircraft engine that combines a jet turbine with a propeller.

UHF - Ultra-high-frequency radio, used for short-range communication (within line of sight), which depends on an aircraft's altitude above the receiving station.

VERTICAL SPEED INDICATOR (VSI) - An instrument that measures in feet per minute an aircraft's rate of climb or descent.

WINDMILL - An in-flight emergency in which the propeller of a shut-down engine fails to feather and continues to spin.

YAW - The flat, sideways turn of an aircraft's nose to the left or right.

YOKE - Sometimes called the control yoke: a device similar to a steering wheel (cut in half), used principally in larger aircraft to control roll and pitch. Moving the yoke sideways activates the ailerons; pushing and pulling the yoke activates the elevators.

photo credits

Pages 1–4 of the photo insert
(Courtesy of Shane Osborn and family)

Damaged EP-3E plane and detail
(Both photographs courtesy of Lockheed Martin Corporation)

Arriving at Hickam Air Force Base
(Courtesy of U.S. Air Force / Technical Sergeant Paul Holcomb)

Awards ceremony at Andrews Air Force Base
(Courtesy of Shane Osborn and family)

Saluting the chairman of the Joint Chiefs of Staff
(Courtesy of U.S. Navy / Photographer's Mate 2nd Class
Bob Houlihan)

Homecoming at Whidbey Island Naval Air Station
(Courtesy of Shane Osborn and family)

The EP-3E crew
(Courtesy of Shane Osborn)

With President Bush
(Courtesy of the White House)

Lieutenant Shane Osborn was born in South Dakota and raised in Nebraska, where he attended the University of Nebraska on a naval ROTC scholarship. Five years after joining the navy, he received the Distinguished Flying Cross medal for heroism and extraordinary achievement in flight. He lives in Anacortes, Washington.

Malcolm McConnell has written extensively on military aviation and is the author of *Fulcrum: A Top-Gun Pilot's Escape from the Soviet Empire.*

Michael French has written several books for young readers, including *Basher Five-Two: The True Story of F-16 Fighter Pilot Captain Scott O'Grady* and the adaptation of *Flags of Our Fathers* by James Bradley and Ron Powers. He lives in New Mexico.